THIS WHERE'S WALLY?
BOOK BELONGS TO:

Robin

ROBIN

Cassidy

First published 2012 by Walker Books Ltd, 87 Vauxhall Walk, London SE11 5HJ

2 4 6 8 10 9 7 5 3

© 2012 Martin Handford

The right of Martin Handford to be identified as author/illustrator of this work has been asserted by him in accordance with the Copyright, Designs and Patents Act 1988

This book has been typeset in Wallyfont and Optima

Printed in China

British Library Cataloguing in Publication Data: a catalogue record for this book is available from the British Library

ISBN 978-1-4063-3662-7

www.walker.co.uk

WHERE'S WALLY?
THE SEARCH FOR THE LOST THINGS

A COMPENDIUM OF PUZZLING PUZZLES

MARTIN HANDFORD

WALKER BOOKS
AND SUBSIDIARIES
LONDON · BOSTON · SYDNEY · AUCKLAND

HI THERE, WALLY FANS!

JOIN ME AND MY FRIENDS WOOF, WENDA, WIZARD WHITEBEARD AND ODLAW ON AN EXTRAORDINARY HUNT FOR OUR LOST THINGS.

WALLY'S KEY

WOOF'S BONE

WENDA'S CAMERA

WIZARD WHITEBEARD'S SCROLL

ODLAW'S BINOCULARS

STRETCH YOUR BRAIN TO ITS LIMITS WITH THE MIND-BOGGLING PUZZLES, AND OTHER INCREDIBLE THINGS TO FIND AND DO ALONG THE WAY.

CRAZY CLOWNS, MONSTROUS BEASTS, MUSICAL MAESTROS, MAGICAL MASTERS AND PLUNDERING PIRATES ARE ALL WAITING TO MEET YOU. AS WELL AS 25 WANDERING WALLY WATCHERS TO FIND.

INVITE YOUR PALS TO HELP IF YOU LIKE AND LET THE SEARCH BEGIN!

Wally

★★ WALLY'S KEY ★ ★

HI FUN-TASTIC FOLLOWERS!

ROLL UP, ROLL UP! ARE YOU READY TO JOIN ME ON MY WILD AND WACKY ADVENTURE? I'VE INVITED MY CRAZY CLOWN FRIENDS ALONG TOO – THEY LOVE PLAYING HIDE AND SEEK, AND ARE ALWAYS UP TO TRICKS!

CAN YOU HELP ME FIND THE FIRST ITEM IN THE SEARCH FOR THE LOST THINGS – MY KEY? BUT, MY RED-NOSED FRIENDS HAVE MADE THE HUNT EVEN MORE CRYPTIC AND DROPPED 25 JOKE KEYS ALL OVER THE PLACE. WHAT A LAUGH!

THE GREAT GAMES START HERE.

Wally

WALLY'S KEY 🔑   JOKE KEY 🗝

TRAVEL ESSENTIALS

Wally is about to set off on his travels. Check
he's carrying everything jotted on his list below and
find all the remaining things in the scene behind.
Bon voyage!

BALLOON
BELT
KETTLE
FLOWER
CUP
MALLET
TOP HAT
SLEEPING BAG
BUCKET
POMPOM
SATCHEL

WALKING STICK
BINOCULARS
RUCKSACK
CAMERA
SPINNING TOP
SNORKEL
CLOCK
SPADE

MORE THINGS TO DO

An anagram is a word where the
order of the letters has been muddled
up. Can you solve these anagrams to
reveal the clown's favourite things?

usdartc epi   Clue: Splat!

dre eons   Clue: Atchoo!

niuylecc   Clue: One big wheel!

DOTTY DOT-TO-DOT

Join up all the dots with *EVEN* numbers to work out what the curiously shaped balloons are floating in the sky.

MORE THINGS TO FIND

☑ Seven custard pies

☑ Eleven blue bow ties

☑ Two clowns wearing the same hat

RED NOSE RUNAROUND

Join up all the red noses, then all the red pompoms
and finally all the red balloons to make a maze. Then find
Wally the *SHORTEST* route to the laughing clowns.

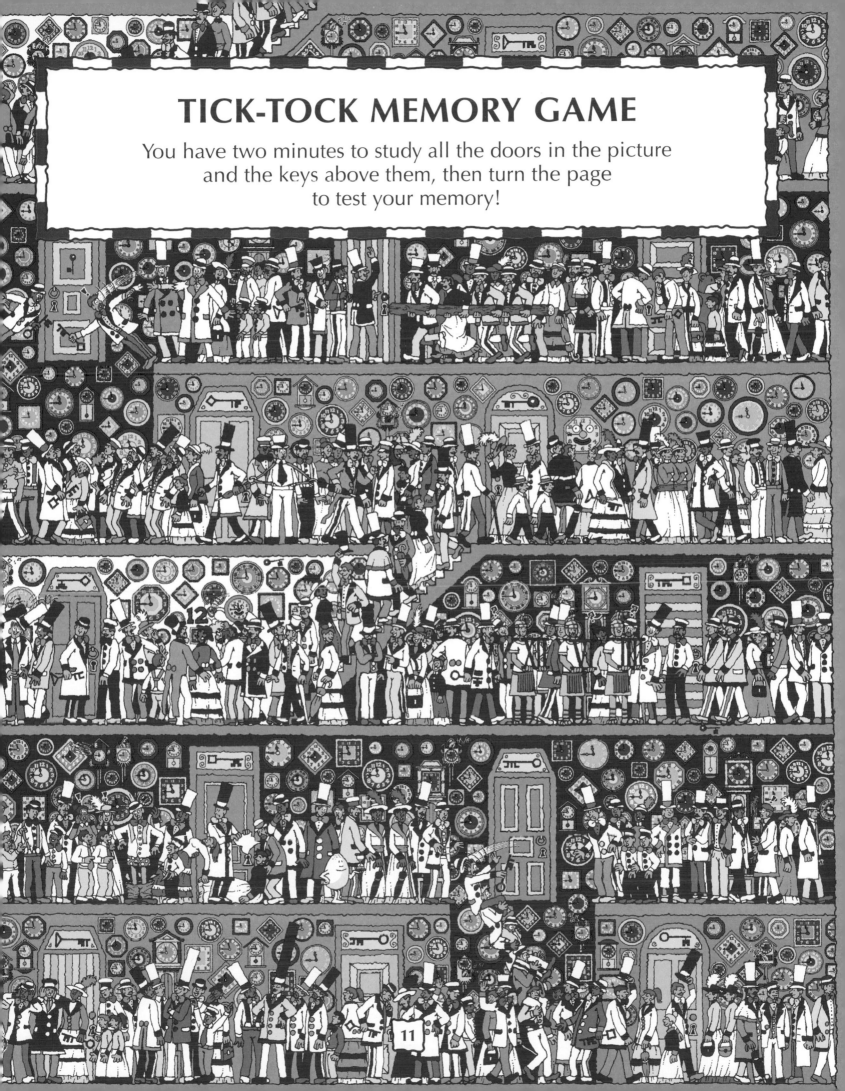

TICK-TOCK MEMORY GAME

You have two minutes to study all the doors in the picture
and the keys above them, then turn the page
to test your memory!

TICK-TOCK MEMORY GAME

Can you remember which key goes above which door
and then draw them in the pictures below?

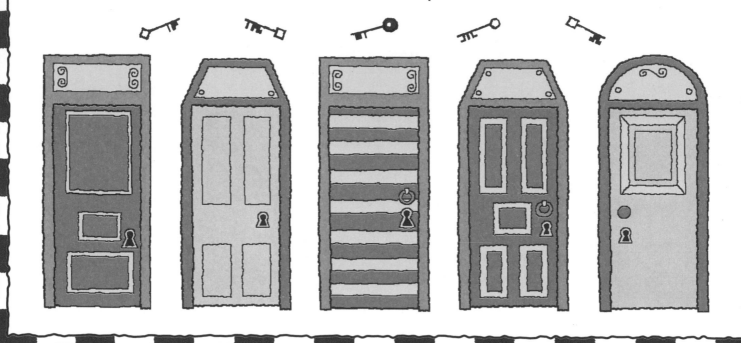

THROUGH THE KEYHOLE GAME

Take your time to peek through these keyholes.
Then turn back the page and find each section in the scene.

HALL OF MIRRORS

Look closely at each of the mirrors. In one mirror Wally is facing in the opposite direction from the other mirrors – can you spot him?

MORE THINGS TO FIND

☐ Four flowers squirting water

☐ A punch-in-the-box

☐ Someone wearing a chef's hat

PYRAMID PUZZLE

Search for the words at the bottom of this page in the pyramid puzzle.
The words go up, down, forwards and backwards –
just like an Egyptian dance!

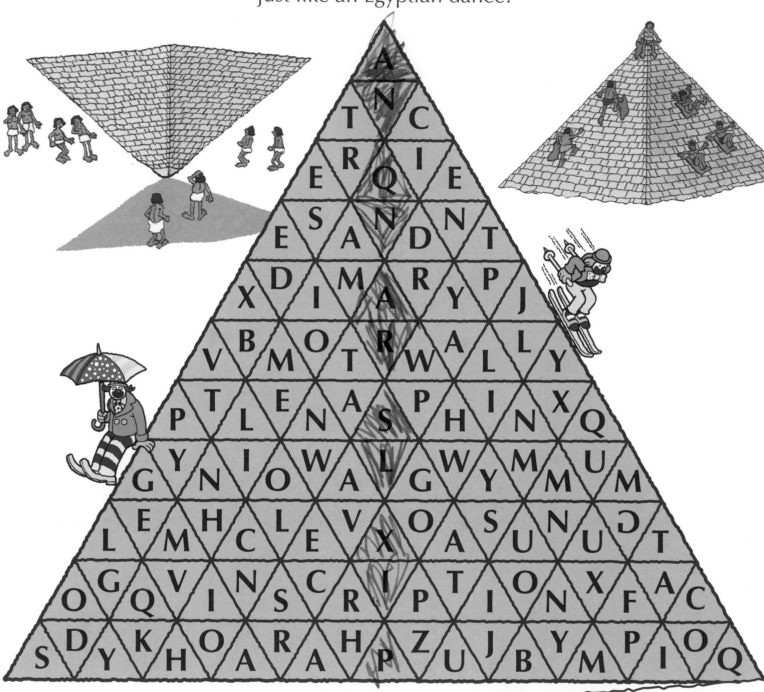

CAT • PYRAMID • SUN • ANCIENT

DESERT • TOMB • WALLY • GODS • PHARAOH

CLOWN • MUMMY • NILE • GOAT • SAND

INSCRIPTION • SLAVE • SPHINX • EGYPT

MORE THINGS TO FIND

How many small triangles in the puzzle?

☐ A back to front letter

☐ A flag with triangles on the opposite page

☐ People sliding on mats later in this chapter

FUNNY FACE FLAGS

Find these foolish faces in the scene below. Can you also find ten clowns playing hide-and-seek?

MORE THINGS TO FIND

☐ Two snakes

☐ A game of noughts and crosses

☐ Ten milk bottles

GAME, SET AND MATCH

Clowns love to play games and laugh out loud! Can you copy
these silly faces in the empty squares below them?

MORE THINGS TO FIND

☑ Two exhausted ball game players

☑ Five red feathers in headbands

☑ A person wearing a red nose

☑ A man wearing clown shoes

MOON MAZE MAYHEM

Help Wally find a path through the moon to reach the red star.

MORE THINGS TO FIND

- ☑ A horseshoe
- ☑ Five green aliens
- ☑ A question mark
- ☑ An exclamation mark

CRAZY KEY HUNT GAME

Photocopy the cards on this page as many times as you like and cut along the dotted edge. Then follow the instructions below and ask your friends to play the game.

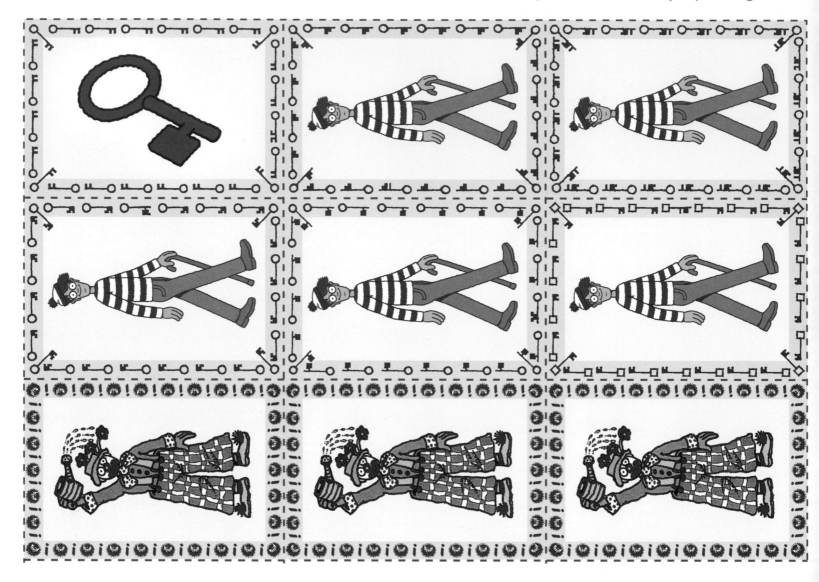

HOW TO PLAY

* To start a trail, hide the card with the key picture.

* Then write a clue to find the key card on the back of a Wally card and hide it.

* Write another Wally card with a clue to where you've hidden the previous one and so on, until all the cards are used up.

 Hide the clown cards somewhere nearby.
When your friends find one, make up a forfeit for them to do before they continue the hunt.

BALLOON BEDLAM

What a terrific tangle! Follow the strings to find out
which balloons Wally and his friends are holding.

MORE THINGS TO DO

Look at the patterns in the border to find a sequence that matches the order of the patterns on the balloons. Then colour in the missing pattern on the empty balloon.

WILD AND WACKY W'S

Can you fit all of the W words in the puzzle? Then *unlock* the three-letter word that doesn't begin with W and find another that has *wandered* backwards.

WAHOO

WAVE

WHOOPEE

WHOOSH

WILD

WONDER

'HIZZ

K--

WITTY

WOW

WISE

'ACKY

REDNAW

SILLY STAMP SNAP

Match each postmark to its stamp by drawing a line between the two. Then draw a design in the blank stamp and write your name inside the empty postmark.

MORE THINGS TO FIND

☐ An upside-down mummy sarcophagus

☐ Six balloons

☐ A ticklish man

CLOWNING AROUND

Yikes! The clowns have muddled up this picture. Guess who it is and put it in the correct order by writing the numbers from 1-6 in the box beside each strip.

MORE THINGS TO DO

Find a famous face in a magazine that is large enough to cut into thick horizontal strips. Then, muddle it up for your friends to solve the puzzle.

HOOPY, LOOPY RIDES

Doodle a fairground ride on the front of this postcard, and write about the amazing things you might be able to see from it on the back.

CONGRATULATIONS, CLEVER CHASERS!

DID YOU REMEMBER TO FIND MY KEY OR DID YOU JUST FIND THE JOKE KEYS? HERE'S A CLUE IF YOU NEED SOME HELP: FIND A CATAPULT AND A CUSTARD PIE ... AND A VERY CHEEKY CLOWN WEARING A GREEN BOW TIE.

GOOD LUCK!

Wally

WALLY'S KEY CHECKLIST

Wait, there's more! Look back over Wally's journey and find...

- ☐ Three pyramid sandcastles
- ☐ A clown with a cone-shaped head
- ☐ Three people talking on walkie talkies
- ☐ A clown hanging on the end of a fishing rod
- ☐ Five sets of twin children
- ☐ A sausage on a fork
- ☐ A clown with a long blue nose
- ☐ A woman wearing a white spotted dress
- ☐ A clock where the cuckoo has escaped
- ☐ Two clocks with clown faces
- ☐ A brown bear
- ☐ A haunted house

Spot one different key in each of the borders of the Wally Crazy Key Hunt cards on page 18.

Which page has the most red noses on it? Don't forget to count the ones on the clowns' faces, but don't include those on the *Red Nose Runaround* maze or the joke keys.

ONE LAST THING...

Four cheeky clowns have wandered into the other chapters, so keep your eyes peeled and see if you can spot them.

Can you find where these pictures come from in Wally's chapter? But beware, there is one picture from elsewhere in the book – it's no joke!

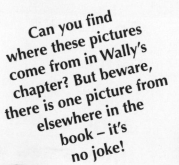

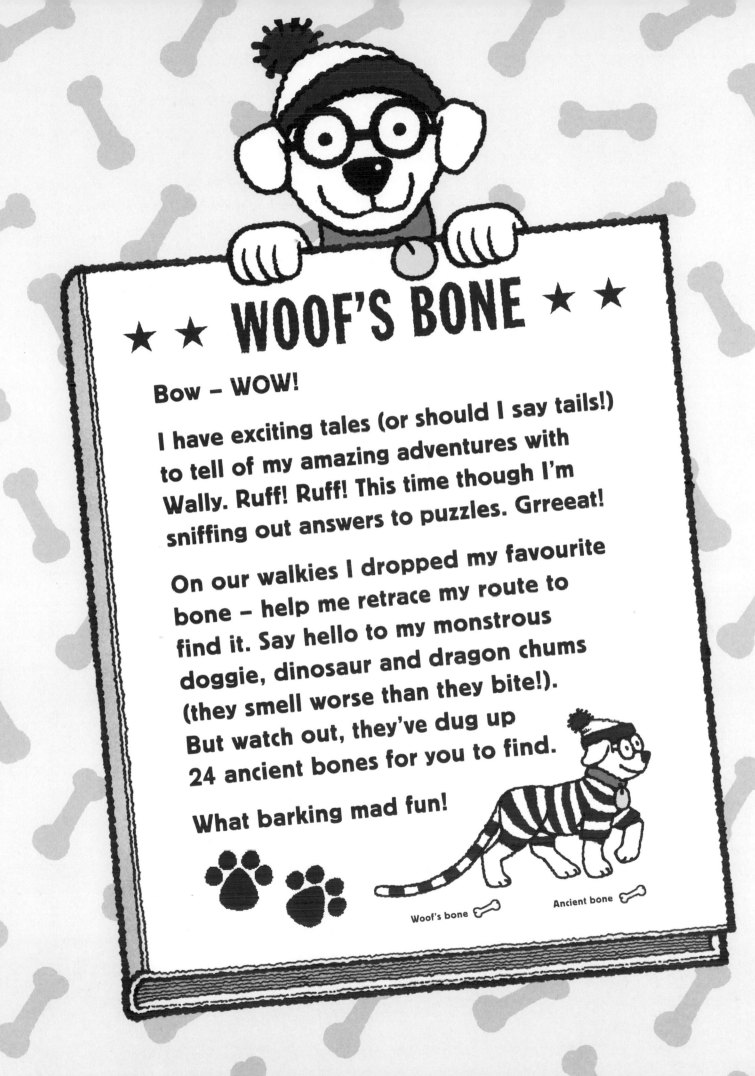

★ ★ WOOF'S BONE ★ ★

Bow – WOW!

I have exciting tales (or should I say tails!) to tell of my amazing adventures with Wally. Ruff! Ruff! This time though I'm sniffing out answers to puzzles. Grreeat!

On our walkies I dropped my favourite bone – help me retrace my route to find it. Say hello to my monstrous doggie, dinosaur and dragon chums (they smell worse than they bite!). But watch out, they've dug up 24 ancient bones for you to find.

What barking mad fun!

Woof's bone 🦴   Ancient bone 🦴

WAG TAIL WAY OUT

Find a way through the maze of Woof tails by only following tails with five red stripes. Start at the square with the red tail and use the guide below to help you reach the square with the white tail.

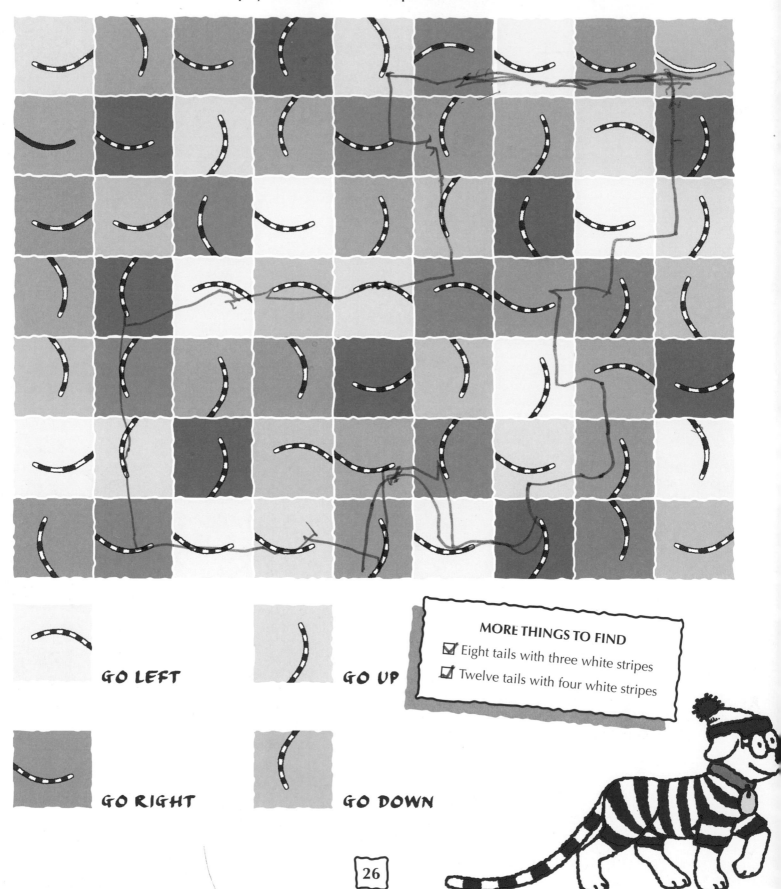

GO LEFT

GO UP

GO RIGHT

GO DOWN

MORE THINGS TO FIND
☑ Eight tails with three white stripes
☑ Twelve tails with four white stripes

MONSTER MADNESS

Can you draw an enormous dog monster in the middle of this scene? Make it as friendly or as terrifying as you like!

MORE THINGS TO DO
* Draw a crest on the white shield
* Find 12 red-handled swords
* Colour in the white plume
* Spot a dinosaur!

WHO'S WHO?

What a mix-up! Unscramble the anagrams and fill in the answers in the boxes next to them. Then draw a line to match the pictures to your answers.

OWOF	Woof
GIMNCIAA	
YALWL	
ALHYW AWCTERL	
VEMCANA	
IPARET	
RIOSNDAU	
CTAROAB	
IGHNKT	
GIKINV	

MORE THINGS TO DO

Write an anagram of your name in the empty box in the left-hand column. Then test your friends!

BARE BONES BRAIN BUSTER

Take your time to study this scene very closely.
Then turn over the page to test your memory.

BARE BONES BRAIN BUSTER

Here goes! How many of these questions can you answer from memory? (It's also fun to guess!) Then turn back the page to see how you did.

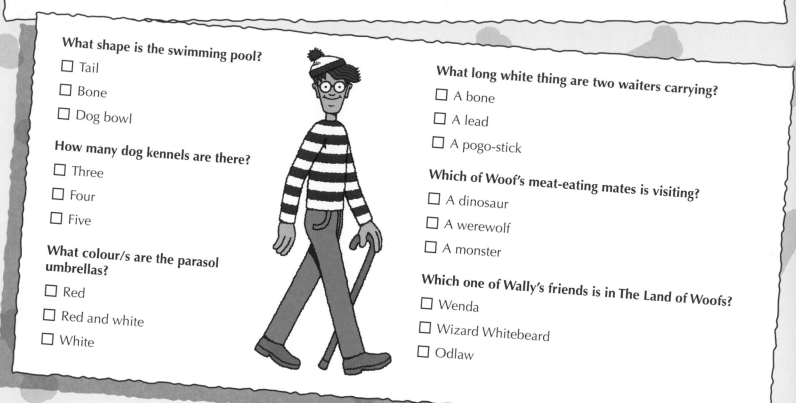

What shape is the swimming pool?

☐ Tail

☐ Bone

☐ Dog bowl

How many dog kennels are there?

☐ Three

☐ Four

☐ Five

What colour/s are the parasol umbrellas?

☐ Red

☐ Red and white

☐ White

What long white thing are two waiters carrying?

☐ A bone

☐ A lead

☐ A pogo-stick

Which of Woof's meat-eating mates is visiting?

☐ A dinosaur

☐ A werewolf

☐ A monster

Which one of Wally's friends is in The Land of Woofs?

☐ Wenda

☐ Wizard Whitebeard

☐ Odlaw

EXTRA BONE-OCULAR EYE-BOGGLER

Study these close-ups carefully and turn back the page to find them.

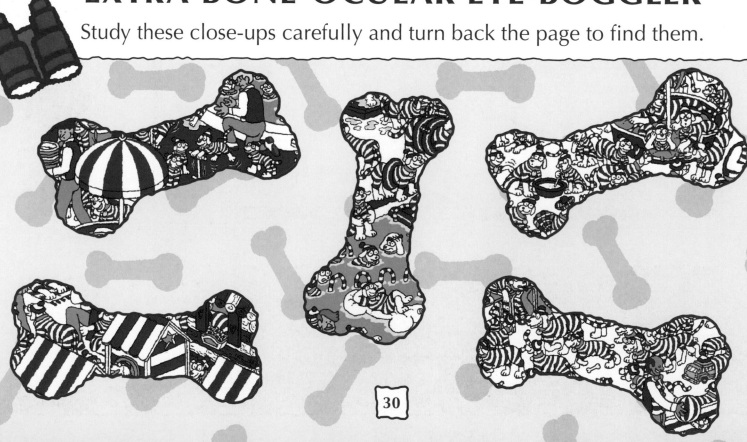

CONNECT THE BONES

Can you join up all nine bones by using only four lines?
You must not lift your pen off the page, but your
lines can go outside of the grid.

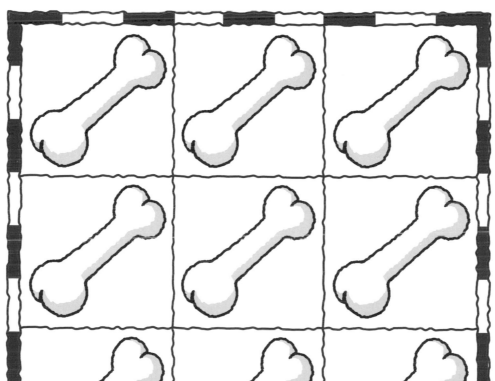
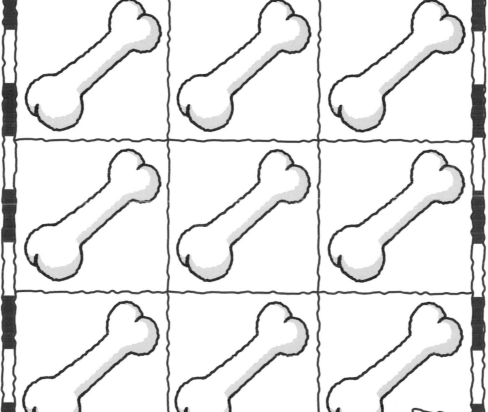

MORE THINGS TO DO

* Join the bones by using two lines.
  You can take your pen off the paper.

* How many squares make up the
  grid? Don't forget that the outer
  box is a square and four grid boxes
  also make up a square!

* Find three of Woof's werewolf
  friends in the pictures.

FLOWER POWER

Can you fill in the missing numbers? Each coloured group of nine squares must contain numbers 1-9, as well as each row that goes up and down or left to right. You may prefer to write in pencil!

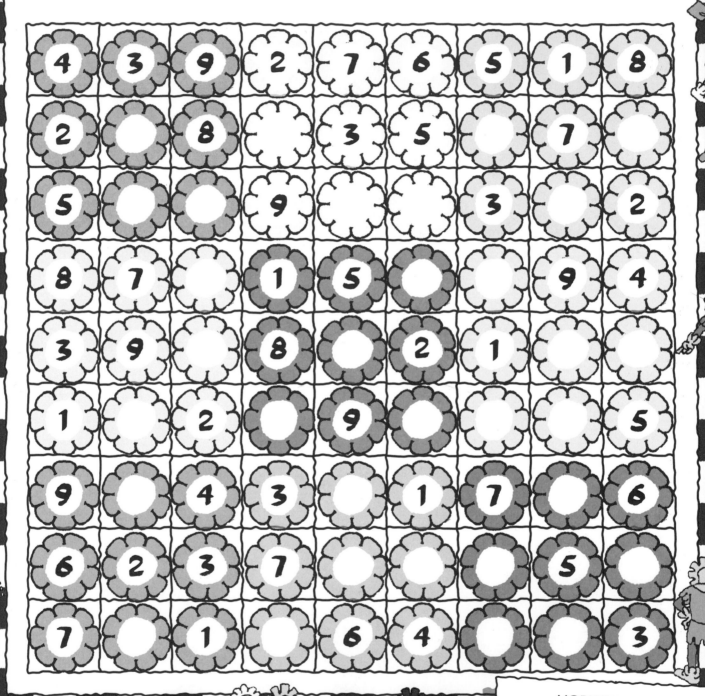

MORE THINGS TO DO

Find these riddles in the picture:

An arrow has sprung a leak,
There's a lot of water, eek!

A man on all fours,
But without Woof-like paws!

BULL'S EYE!

Help Woof reach the target in the centre of the maze by passing all five of his dog pals but avoiding the bulls. It's a-maze-ing!

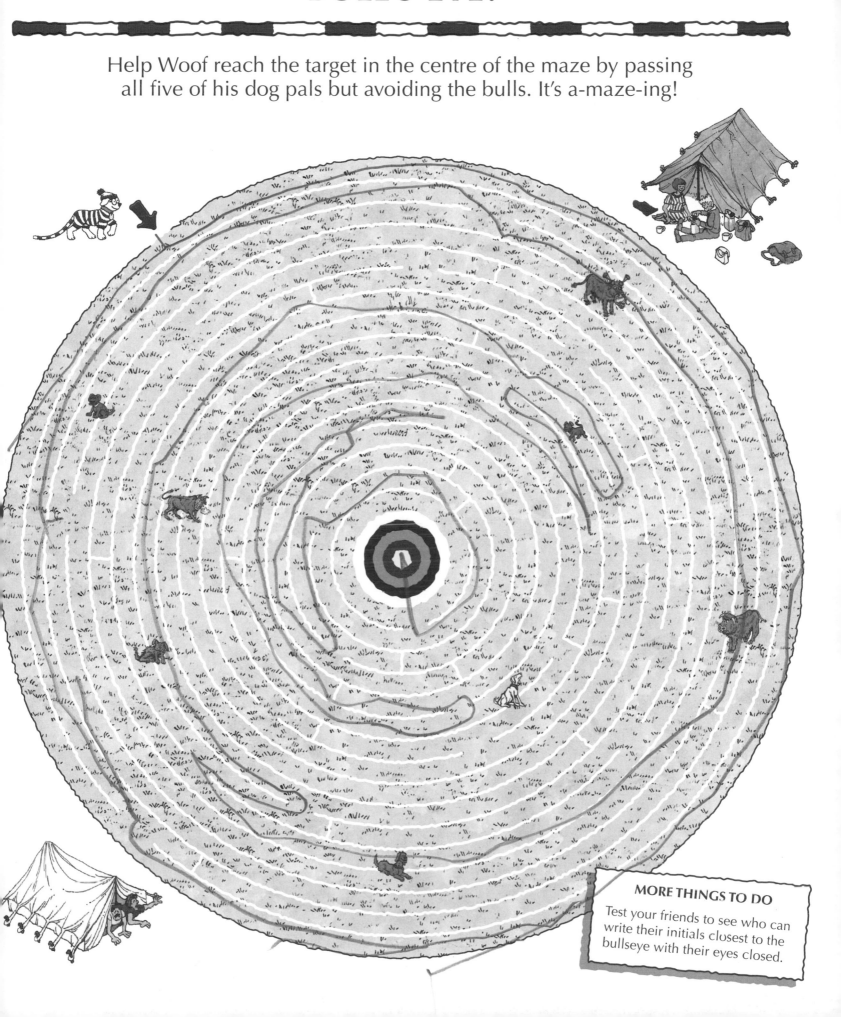

MORE THINGS TO DO

Test your friends to see who can write their initials closest to the bullseye with their eyes closed.

WOOF'S WORD WHEEL

Use the clues to help you find five words using three or more letters in the word wheel. Every answer must contain the letter O only once.

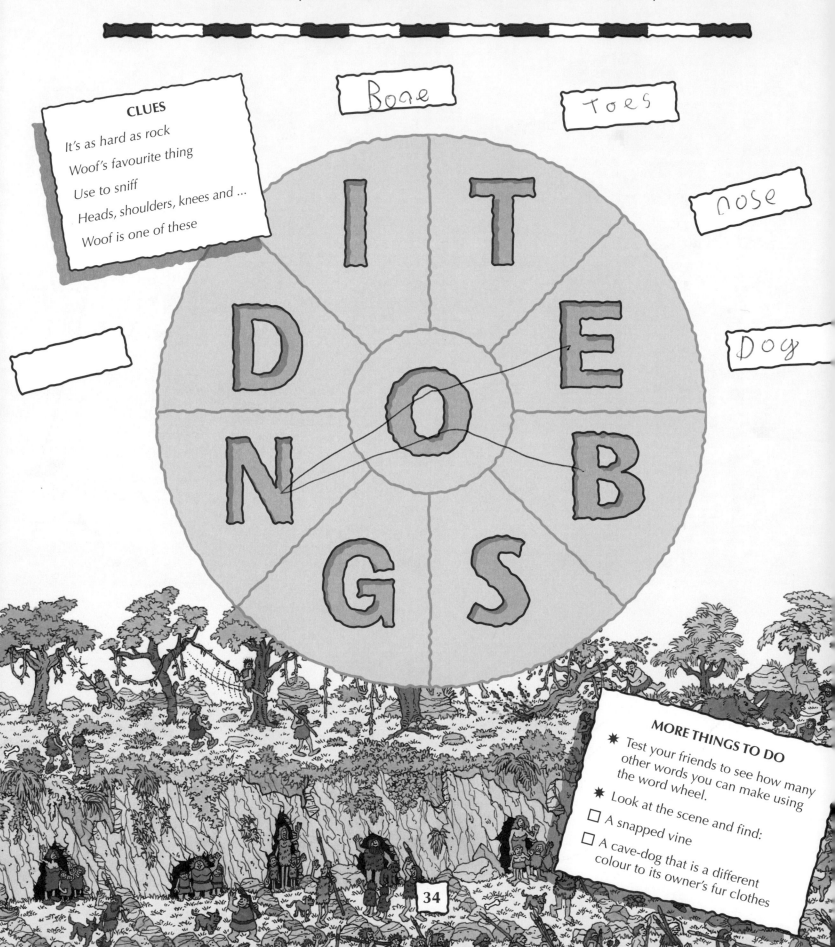

CLUES

It's as hard as rock

Woof's favourite thing

Use to sniff

Heads, shoulders, knees and ...

Woof is one of these

Bone

Toes

nose

Dog

I T

D E

O

N B

G S

MORE THINGS TO DO

★ Test your friends to see how many other words you can make using the word wheel.

★ Look at the scene and find:

☐ A snapped vine

☐ A cave-dog that is a different colour to its owner's fur clothes

TRUTH OR TAILS?

Test your knowledge of Woof's four-legged ancient friends and work out which questions are true and which are false.

1. Dinosaurs ruled the earth for 160 million years.

2. The correct way to spell this dinosaur's name is: Parasawralophus.

3. The Brachiosaurus had a very long neck.

4. The Ichthyosaurus was an under-water sea creature and is the relative of a shark.

5. The difference between a herbivore and a carnivore was the colour of their scales.

6. This anagram spells a dinosaur's name: uyaxntoarrunsres.

7. The Ankylosaurus had a club tail.

8. A Pterodactyl had three wings.

9. Triceratops dinosaurs had a bony frill.

10. There was a dinosaur called Diplodocus.

Use the Internet or an encyclopaedia to help you, or look up more fun facts about dinosaurs.

Did you know?

There was a dinosaur similar to a dog! It is called Cynognathus (*sy-nog-nay-thus*) and was a hairy mammal-like animal with dog-like teeth. Woof claims that his great-great-great grandfather was one (calculated in dog years, of course)!

ONE MORE THING!

What is the name of the dinosaur whose skeleton is in this picture? *Clue: it begins with the letter 'S'.*

BURIED BONES

Woof has been busy burying bones! Can you fill in the grid coordinates for the items at the bottom of the page that mark where he has hidden them?

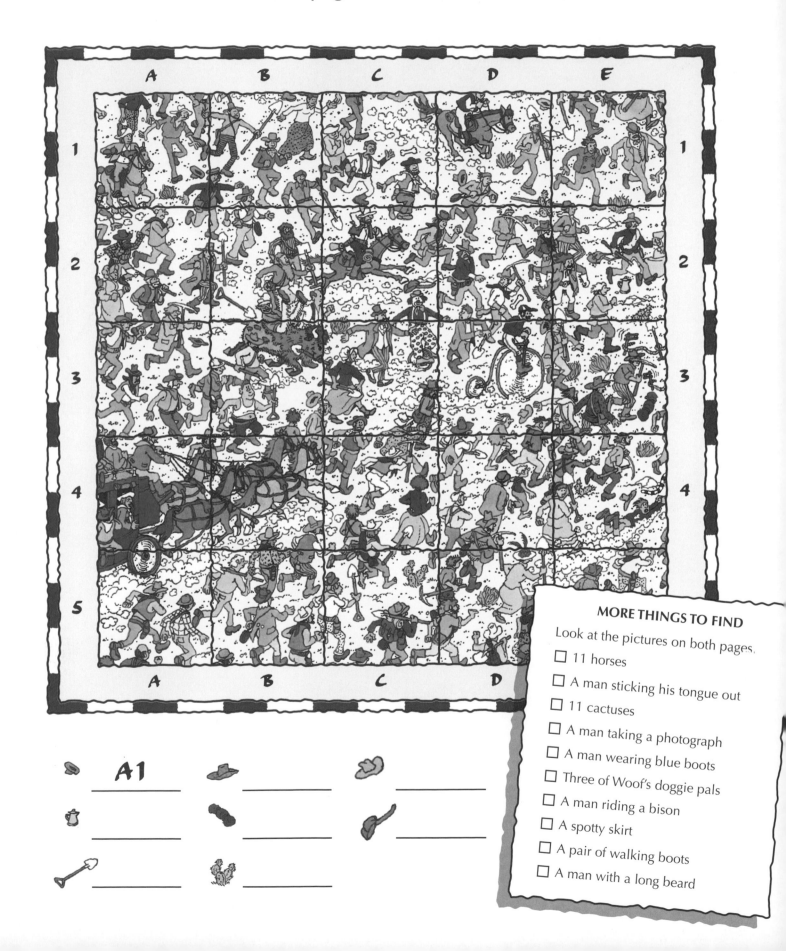

A1

MORE THINGS TO FIND

Look at the pictures on both pages.

☐ 11 horses

☐ A man sticking his tongue out

☐ 11 cactuses

☐ A man taking a photograph

☐ A man wearing blue boots

☐ Three of Woof's doggie pals

☐ A man riding a bison

☐ A spotty skirt

☐ A pair of walking boots

☐ A man with a long beard

DIGGING FOR GOLD

Yee-haw! The answers to this crossword puzzle are set in the wild, wild west.

Across

1. A large farm used to keep animals (5 letters)

3. The seat placed on a horse's back (6 letters)

4. Vessel with handle used to carry water (6 letters)

6. Someone who bends metal and mends horseshoes (10 letters)

9. The opposite to cold (3 letters)

10. A tool used to dig. Pick... (3 letters)

11. Midday (4 letters)

Down

1. To steal (3 letters)

2. Money offered on a poster for a wanted person (6 letters)

3. A rush of startled animals (8 letters)

5. A green plant with spikes (6 letters)

7. A looped rope used to catch horses (5 letters)

8. A mode of transport with carriages (5 letters)

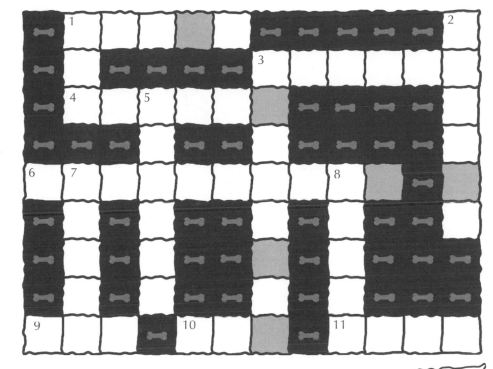

MORE THINGS TO DO

There are six letters in grey squares in the crossword puzzle. Can you unscramble the anagram to spell out grid coordinates and find where Woof has buried some gold coins? The answer will be a letter and a number spelt in letters.

_____ / _____

NUMBER CRUNCHING

Solve the number puzzle to help Woof jump down through the clouds.
Subtract 1 from any red number and add 1 to any blue number. Then draw a path
to the finish by connecting up eleven clouds which add up to the number 5.

Start

Finish

MORE THINGS TO DO
* Find a sailor with a blue beard
* Find eight green dragons
* Which cloud has the highest final total?

DOG'S DINNER

Scribble out all the Ws to decode Woof's letter and write the answer in the spaces above each line. A double W means a break between words.

W.LWEWAWDWY,WWSWTWEWAWDWY,WWGWO!
W'VTWHWEWWRWAWCWEWWIWSWWOWNW!
WWMWEWWAWNWDWWMWYWWCWAWNWI
WNWEWWFWRWIWEWNWDWSWWAWRWEW
WCWHWAWSWIWNWGWWOWUWRWWFWAWV
L'OWUWRWIWTWEWWFWOWOWDWWGWRWOWU
^JPWS-SWAWUWSWAWGWEWS,WWBWOWNWEWS,
^JWCWAWTWSWWAWNWDWWEWWVWEWNWWP
^VOWSWTWMWEWN!

MORE THINGS TO FIND
☐ 31 envelopes
☐ A dog who is not wearing a collar
☐ Two blue dog bowls
☐ A cat dressed as Woof

How many 'wow' words are in Woof's unscrambled letter?

BITES & PIECES

Which three pieces are missing from the jigsaw? You have five pieces to choose from, so study each carefully.

MORE THINGS TO FIND

☐ A dog-man holding two bones

☐ A cat on wheels

☐ A man dressed as a poodle

PLAY BALL

Can you work out which rocks come next in these four sequences?
Draw the size of the rocks first, then colour them in.

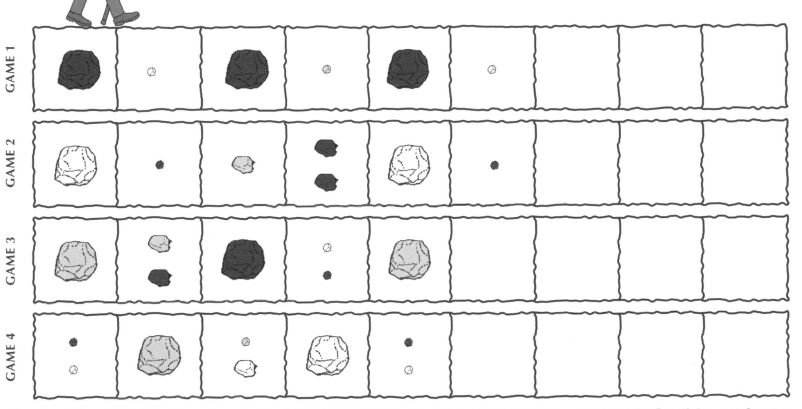

GAME 1

GAME 2

GAME 3

GAME 4

MORE THINGS TO FIND

☐ Ten blue-and-white striped dinosaurs

☐ A dinosaur with a blue horn

☐ Two red dinosaurs hiding under a pink dinosaur

What a gnashing set of tricky trials Wally-Watchers –
you really are top-dogs!

Did you fetch my beloved bone, or were you distracted by
the ancient ones? I've retrieved this clue to help you find its
whereabouts: sniff out six furry boots and you'll be hot on
the tail of my lost bone.

Thanks cheery champions!

Can you spot these
pictures somewhere
in Woof's chapter?
But hold your horses,
one picture is from
a different place
entirely!

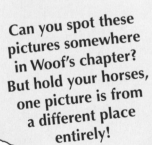

WOOF'S BONE CHECKLIST

Pad back through Woof's wonderful wanders
and find…

- [ ] Seven red dog bowls
- [ ] A wanted poster
- [ ] A blue horse
- [ ] A dog-man throwing a stick
- [ ] A rabbit being pulled from a hat
- [ ] Four Woofs with bowls on their heads
- [ ] A man riding a bull backwards
- [ ] A red and pink striped dinosaur
- [ ] Three sheep
- [ ] A man sticking his tongue out at a green dragon
- [ ] Four flying bats
- [ ] Three escaping criminals
- [ ] A hedge in the shape of a watering can
- [ ] A woman wearing a fur coat

ONE LAST THING…

Look out for many more of Woof's
doggie pals in the rest of this book.
How many can you count along
the way?

★ WENDA'S CAMERA ★

WELCOME SHARP-EYED SEEKERS, TO AN ALL-SINGING, ALL-DANCING MEGA MUSICAL SHOW!

MY FRIENDS FROM THE CREW TOOK ME ON A TOUR BEHIND THE SCENES AND I'VE MISPLACED MY WONDERFUL CAMERA. DOY-RAY-ME, THAT WON'T DO!

LET'S GET TO IT! TUNE YOUR BRAIN INTO THE MELODIC MAYHEM OF THE PUZZLES AND HELP BRING ME ONE STEP CLOSER TO MY PRECIOUS POSSESSION. OH, AND THERE ARE 18 OF THE CREW'S RED CAMERAS TO TRACK DOWN TOO.

TAP, TAP! CLAP, CLAP! DON'T MISS A BEAT!

WENDA

WENDA'S CAMERA   CREW'S CAMERA

SNAPPY SINGING!

These stamping feet are creating cracks everywhere in this spectacular singing scene. Can you find eight broken things from the list below?

BROKEN THINGS TO FIND
- [ ] A smashed mirror
- [ ] Woof's snapped bone
- [ ] A bent umbrella
- [ ] A broken walking stick
- [ ] A split stage
- [ ] A cracked clapper board
- [ ] A ladder with a broken rung
- [ ] Wenda's broken spectacles

MUSICAL FRAME FUN

Wenda has framed her favourite musical photographs. Can you find a picture that doesn't contain a musical note, and one frame with Wenda's face in the border?

MORE THINGS TO FIND
- ☐ Twelve violins
- ☐ A large bow tie
- ☐ A guitar
- ☐ Three tubas
- ☐ A one-eyed man

CAMERA CLOSE-UPS

Whoops, Wenda's camera is broken! Can you work out who she has accidentally zoomed into? Some people appear more than once.

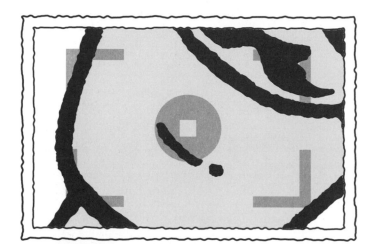

MORE THINGS TO DO

Experiment with your own crazy close-ups using the zoom on a camera or a mobile phone.

BUSY BANDSTAND

What a musical muddle! Look at the clapper board and match up the instruments or person with the items needed to play music in a band.

DRUM
CLARINET
CONDUCTOR
TROMBONE
VIOLIN
TRIANGLE
PIANO

MOUTHPIECE
BOW
KEYS
ROD
BATON
REED
STICKS

Rearrange the words below to make the title of Wenda's favourite song. The band is supposed to be rehearsing it!

A Wonderland Walking in Winter

MORE THINGS TO DO

* Find animal costumes in the scene beginning with B, C, P and two beginning with R?

* Sing your favourite song!

A COLOURFUL TUNE

Can you find these sets of musical notes inside the puzzle?
The answers run across, down and diagonally.

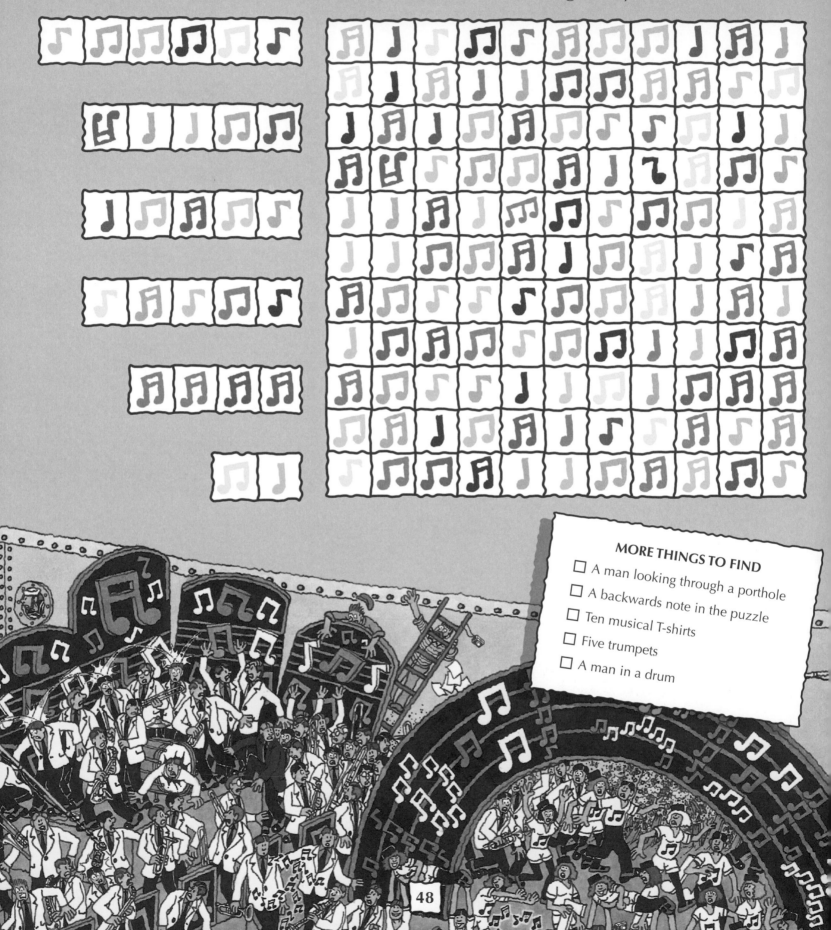

MORE THINGS TO FIND
- ☐ A man looking through a porthole
- ☐ A backwards note in the puzzle
- ☐ Ten musical T-shirts
- ☐ Five trumpets
- ☐ A man in a drum

LOST LUGGAGE

Spot Wenda and the crew's lost luggage in these photographs. Wenda's bag has a red-and-white striped luggage label, and the crew's bags have seven yellow and two blue ones.

MORE THINGS TO FIND
- ☐ A bag with a red luggage label
- ☐ A man wearing a green tie
- ☐ A woman wearing yellow shoes
- ☐ A barre
- ☐ Two white luggage labels

WOBBLY WORD LADDERS

Hang on! Can you fill in the missing words in these ladders?
Start at the top and work your way down by changing one letter at
a time, but keeping the rest of the letters in the same order.

WOW

DOT

SONG

FIND

MORE THINGS TO FIND

☐ A hat with a red bobble

☐ A parrot

☐ Someone sticking out their tongue

Solve the riddle to find the person:

Looking through my hand-held glasses,
I can see closely all that passes

REELY-FUN

Study the tiny pictures in the sprockets of the film reels and find all the people and things (but not the stars) in the large pictures.

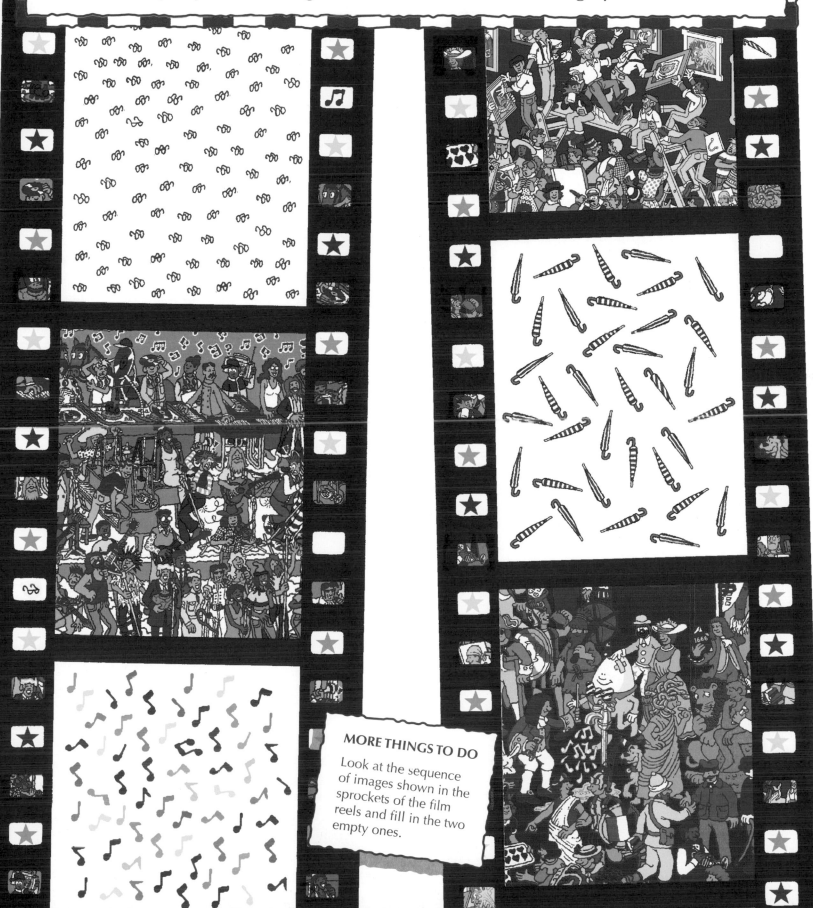

MORE THINGS TO DO

Look at the sequence of images shown in the sprockets of the film reels and fill in the two empty ones.

BEHIND THE SCENES

Oh no, Wenda's photographs have all printed out in funny colours!
Only two of these pictures are from the same musical scene –
can you work out which ones?

MORE THINGS TO DO

Write the names of three colours in different coloured pens (e.g. the word yellow in green pen). Then ask a friend to quickly say what colour the word is written in. Do they always say the colour the word spells?

COSTUME COSTS

Wenda has given you £15 to spend in the sales. You need to buy one or more of these items, but you can only buy one hat. Remember to take away the discount from the full price. You must spend all of your money!

Hats £3 (£2 off)   Ties £3 (£1 off)

Shirts £10 (£7 off)   Jackets £10 (£6 off)

£_____
+ £_____
+ £_____
+ £_____
+ £_____
+ £_____
= £15

MORE THINGS TO DO

✷ Colour in the Wenda pound notes.

✷ Find twelve other Wenda pound notes in the scene.

54

BOX BAMBOOZLE

Take a close look at the design on Wenda's unfolded camera box. Which of the three boxes match the unfolded box? It's a crazily clever combination!

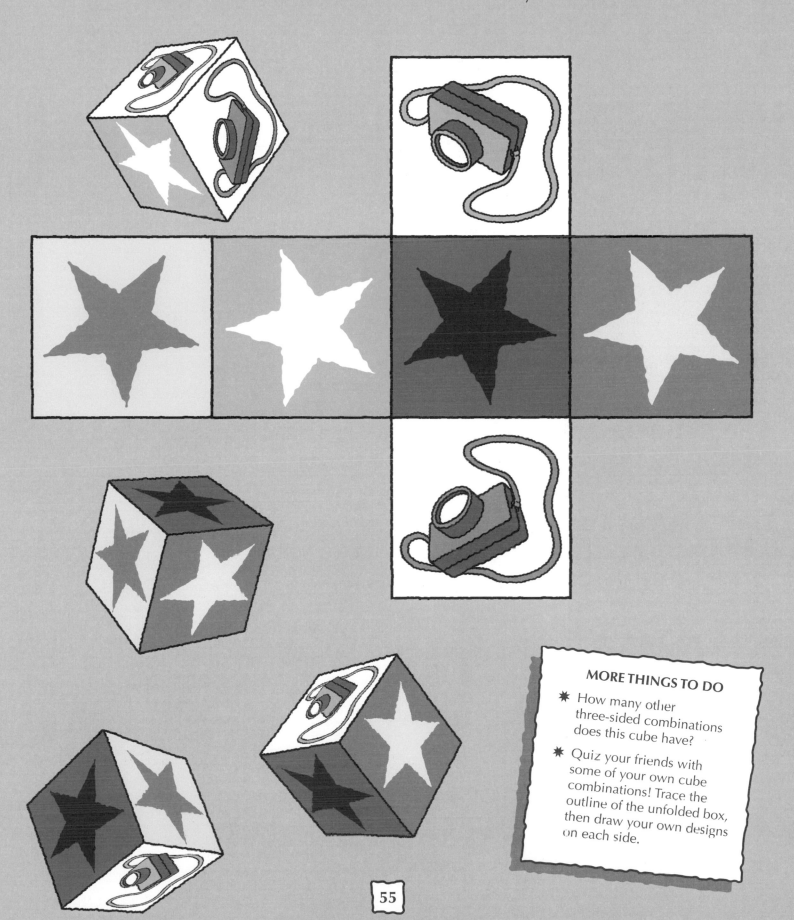

MORE THINGS TO DO

* How many other three-sided combinations does this cube have?

* Quiz your friends with some of your own cube combinations! Trace the outline of the unfolded box, then draw your own designs on each side.

OH CRUMBS!

It's teatime back-stage! Unscramble all the ingredients for this cake recipe by scribbling out the letters in grey that spell 'camera' in every word.

CEAGMGESRA

CBAUMTETREAR

SCELF ARAISMINEG FRLOAUR

CHOCCAOLAMTEE CRHIPAS

ICCINAG MSEUGRARA

RCEAD MCHEERRRIEAS

CCUSATMAERRDA

MORE THINGS TO FIND

☐ A gingerbread man

☐ Wenda's cake with three red stripes

☐ A double-ended wooden spoon

56

UNDER THE SPOTLIGHT

Lights, camera, action! Can you spot ten differences between these two musical stage scenes?

MORE THINGS TO DO

Create your own checklist of things to find in the scenes.

- ☐ ....
- ☐ ....
- ☐ ....
- ☐ ....
- ☐ ....
- ☐ ....

WHAT AN EXPRESSION!

Wenda loves catching people unawares in her photographs! Doodle and colour in the empty frames and faces to make your own mini portraits.

DANCING SILHOUETTES

Wenda has sent you a postcard from the after show party.
Match the silhouettes with her funky stepping friends on the dance floor.

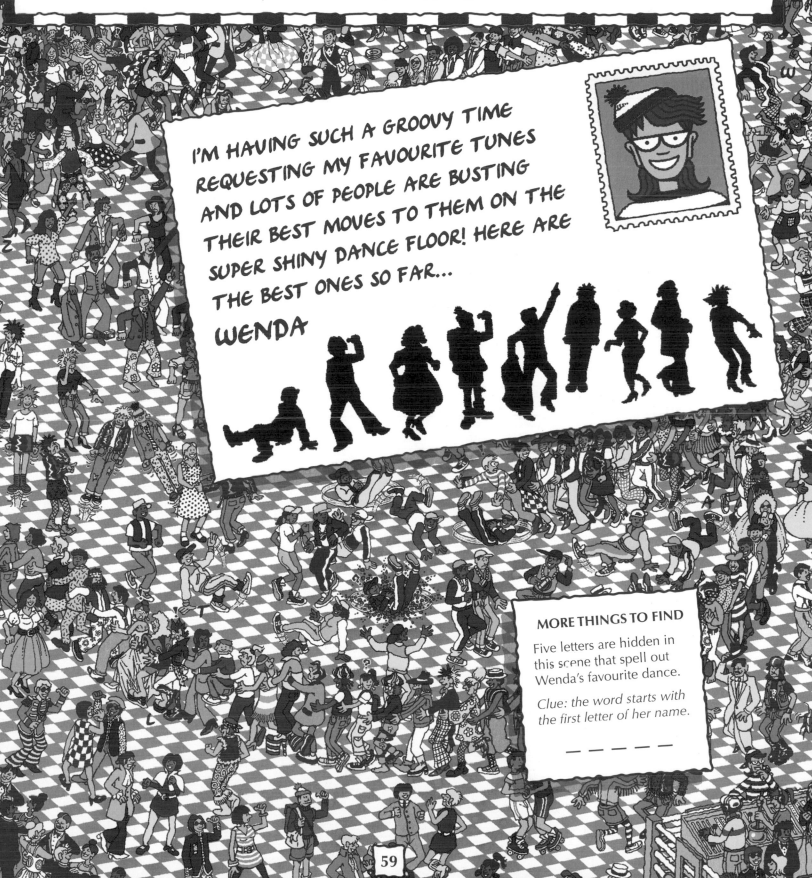

I'M HAVING SUCH A GROOVY TIME REQUESTING MY FAVOURITE TUNES AND LOTS OF PEOPLE ARE BUSTING THEIR BEST MOVES TO THEM ON THE SUPER SHINY DANCE FLOOR! HERE ARE THE BEST ONES SO FAR...

WENDA

MORE THINGS TO FIND

Five letters are hidden in this scene that spell out Wenda's favourite dance.

Clue: the word starts with the first letter of her name.

— — — — —

WELL, I THINK YOU EARNED YOUR STRIPES AND DIDN'T MAKE TOO MANY 'SNAPPY' DECISIONS. DID YOU FIND MY CAMERA, SEEKERS? HERE'S A CLUE AND I'M SURE YOUR FRIENDS WILL 'LENS' A HAND IF YOU NEED IT: LOOK FOR A TINY HOUSE THAT'S TOO SWEET TO LIVE IN...

BRAVO! ENCORE!

WENDA

Enjoy searching for these pictures in Wenda's chapter. Watch that you don't spend too long looking for one of them, because it's from a different chapter!

WENDA'S CAMERA CHECKLIST

Flick back through Wenda's extravaganza and find...

- ☐ Seven film cans
- ☐ Two Wendas wearing blue shoes
- ☐ A frame within a frame
- ☐ A man with his head stuck in a tap
- ☐ Frankenstein's monster
- ☐ 23 ladders
- ☐ A rabbit man playing the drums with carrots
- ☐ A couple wearing roller skates
- ☐ A yellow Woof
- ☐ A musical tap
- ☐ A man painting a nose
- ☐ Four green striped umbrellas
- ☐ A man wearing five hats
- ☐ An Odlaw wearing a red bobble hat

Which page has the most number of musical notes on it, not including page 48?

ONE LAST THING...

Did you spot nine people holding sheets of white paper during Wenda's adventure? These are the crew's lost music sheets, so if you haven't found them yet, keep looking!

STARS AND STRIPES

Which stripy path leads from Wizard Whitebeard's seal to his star? You better get there quickly as his spell is making multiple Wallies!

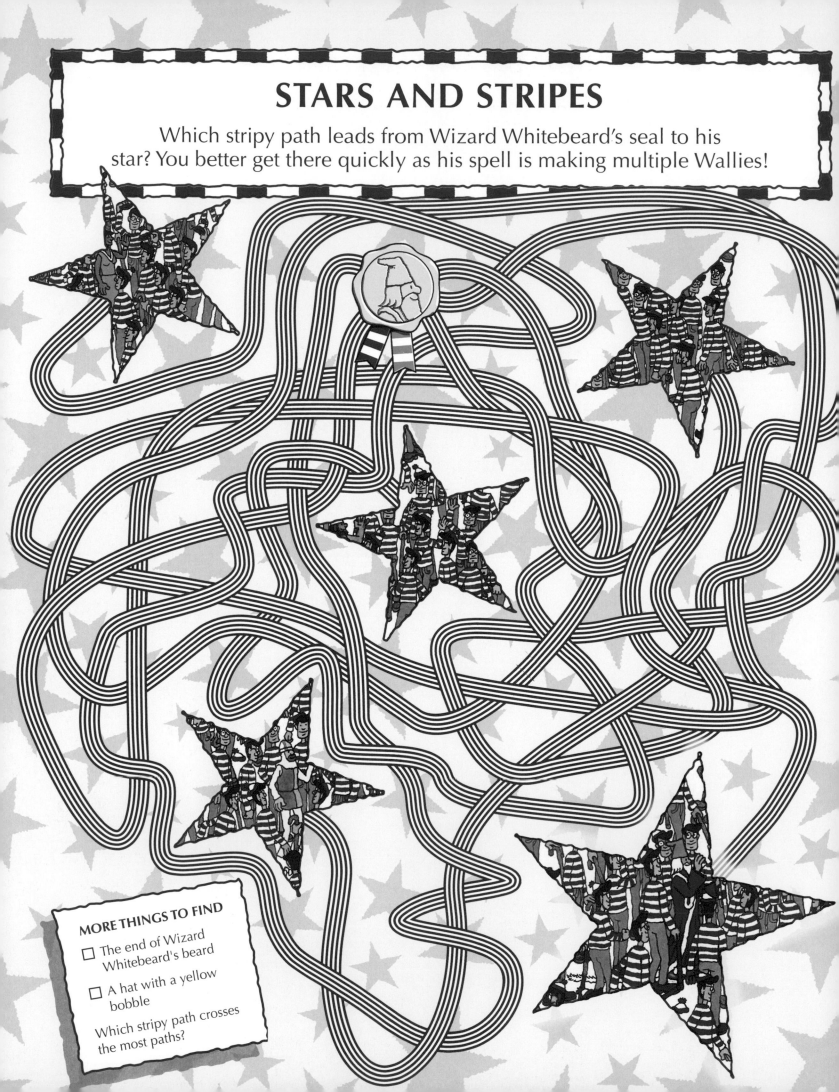

MORE THINGS TO FIND

☐ The end of Wizard Whitebeard's beard

☐ A hat with a yellow bobble

Which stripy path crosses the most paths?

SOMETHING FISHY

Match up the sets of three identically coloured fish. One fish is not part of a set, so have a splish-splashing time finding out which one!

MORE THINGS TO FIND

- [ ] A smiling fish
- [ ] An angry fish
- [ ] A fish with closed eyes

SPELL-TACULAR!

These four words have stretched out in a spectacular star shape.
Can you train your eyes to read them?

START HERE!

MORE THINGS TO FIND
- [ ] A white suitcase
- [ ] A stripy rocket
- [ ] A green wellington boot
- [ ] A frog

Clue: hold the book in front of your nose and tilt it backwards. Read the word in front of you, then turn the book to the right and read the next word and so on.

GIANT GAME

Start on the board game square next to each player's picture.
Then follow their footstep guide to work out who picks up the scroll.

MORE THINGS TO FIND
- [ ] Nine men wearing helmets
- [ ] Someone wearing blue and yellow tights
- [ ] Four pitch forks

MIX-UP MADNESS

What a muddle! Match the top halves of these characters
to the correct bottom halves.

MORE THINGS TO DO

* Draw your own fantasy characters in the two blank boxes! Flick through the book for inspiration for a top half and a bottom half.

* Give some of the mixed-up characters combination names e.g. Vikingator (viking + gladiator).

TWO BY TWO

Wizard Whitebeard is helping Noah get pairs of animals on to his ark. Join up the numbered red dots to reveal a creature that wants to travel alone.

MORE THINGS TO FIND
- [ ] An elephant shaped tree
- [ ] Another Noah's ark in this chapter
- [ ] A bird's nest

WORD CASTLE

Find the words at the bottom of this page in the three-letter bricks of this castle. A word can read across more than one brick.

R O F		A R A	M I D		A X E
M X A		J O P	W W O		W G R
L W A	D R A	W B R	I D G E	H L	D R A
F L A	G L V	N E K	R C A	T A P	U L T
N T P	C A S	T L E	L Q P	U F M	P X E
W Q T	E U F	Y U X	H D A	B A T	T L E
M O A	T H Y	K W S	E J I	U L E	I A F
D G E	M I L	A I N	S I F	O R T	A F R
A R R	O W H	R E E	A K L	K C E	T L H
H F M	A R A	W N P	M T L	H F L	A G T
W A L	L T O	H Y O	E A B	O W P	P C G

MORE THINGS TO FIND

☐ A word that features twice in the puzzle

☐ Two magic words that can open the castle drawbridge.

Clue: ten letters that go up, across and down.

O _ _ _ _ / _ _ S _ _ E

BOW
WALL
MOAT
ARROW
CASTLE
DRAWBRIDGE

CATAPULT
RAM
FORT
AXE
BATTLE
FLAG

SHIELDS AND STAVES

On guard, eyes at the ready! Find two pictures that are the same.

MORE THINGS TO FIND

Which colour frames are there most of?

☐ Four blue shields

☐ Eight green hats

☐ A carved red staff

☐ A man with stars above his head

GENIE-OUS!

Draw in the missing symbols to release the genie from its lamp!
All nine symbols must appear once in each box,
but never in the same row.

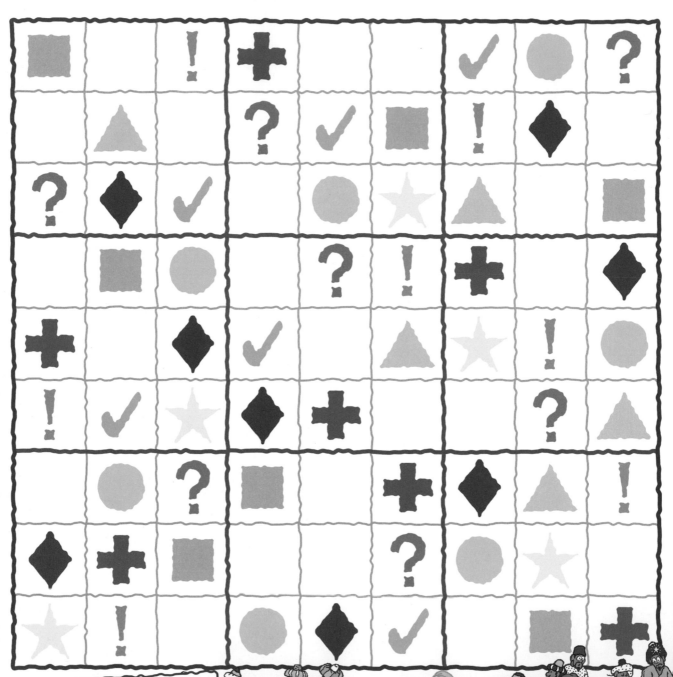

MORE THINGS TO DO

If you were granted three wishes, what would they be?

1. ....

2. ....

3. ....

DOUBLE VISION

All is not what it seems with these magic monks and red-cloaked ghouls.
Spot six differences in one of the scenes.

FRUIT SQUASH

Study the fruit in the puzzle closely – to the left and right, above and below. There are two *zesty* fruit which are always next to each other. Can you draw them in the empty squares?

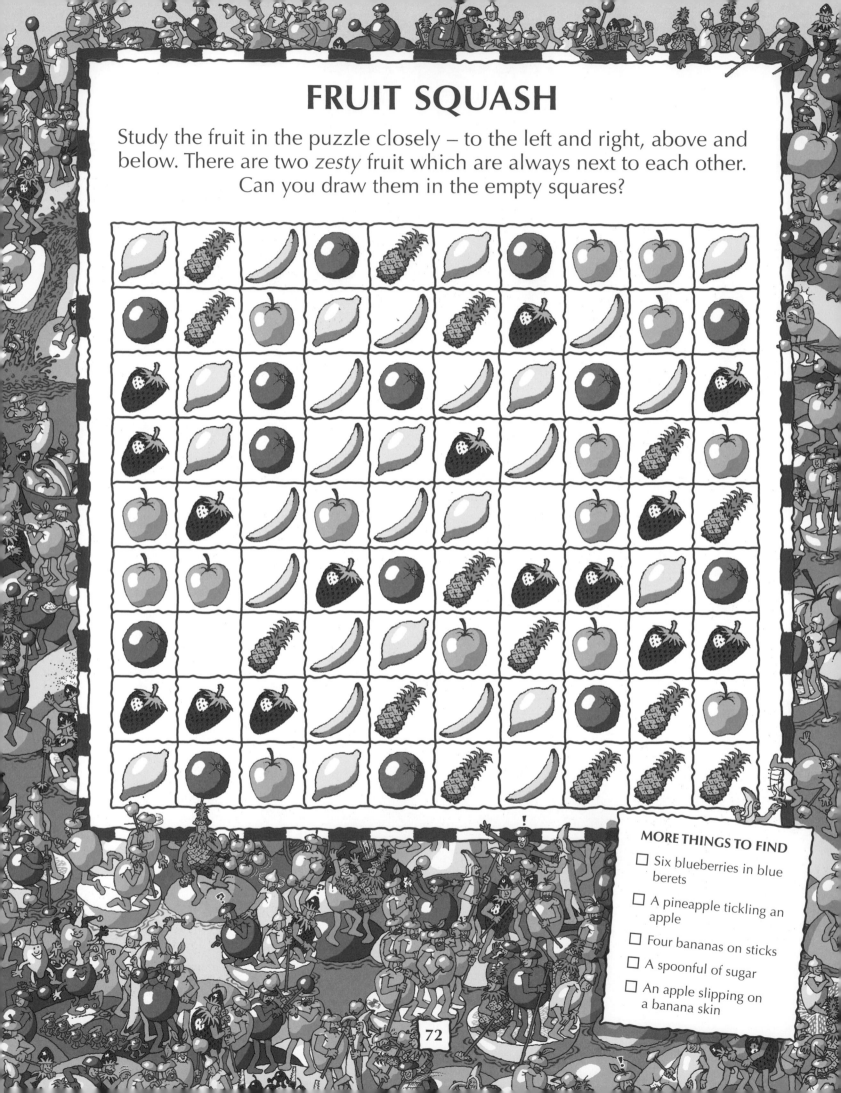

MORE THINGS TO FIND

- ☐ Six blueberries in blue berets
- ☐ A pineapple tickling an apple
- ☐ Four bananas on sticks
- ☐ A spoonful of sugar
- ☐ An apple slipping on a banana skin

DRAGON DELIGHT

A magical dragon flying competition is about to begin. Draw lots of other dragon contestants to take part in it!

MORE THINGS TO DO

Choose your favourite dragon (it might be one that you have drawn) and give it a name. What do you think its eggs look like and what is its favourite food?

Look at the picture and find:

☐ A dragon with a very long tail

☐ A dragon egg

☐ A red spotty bag on a stick

73

HAT TRICK

Wow! Pow! Kazam! Draw tiny people underneath
the hats to create your own scene.

WHICH WITCH IS WHICH?

Read the witchy riddles and match them to the pictures.

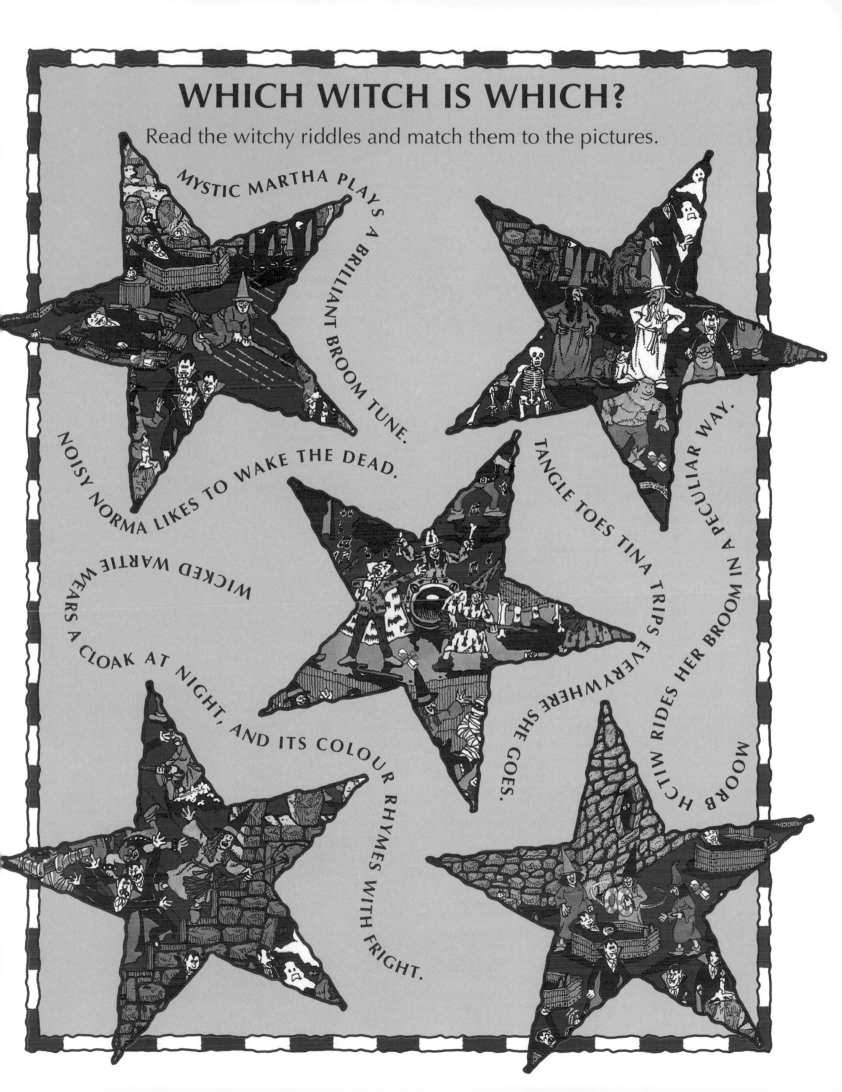

MYSTIC MARTHA PLAYS A BRILLIANT BROOM TUNE.

NOISY NORMA LIKES TO WAKE THE DEAD.

TANGLE TOES TINA TRIPS EVERYWHERE SHE GOES.

WICKED WARTIE WEARS A CLOAK AT NIGHT, AND ITS COLOUR RHYMES WITH FRIGHT.

WITCH BRENDA RIDES HER BROOM IN A PECULIAR WAY.

MAGIC NUMBER

Cross out the numbers in the border matching these descriptions and reveal a magic number to be used later…

☆ **Number sevens**

☆ **Two numbers next to each other that are the same**

☆ **Two numbers next to each other that add up to ten**

☆ **Even numbers**

MORE THINGS TO FIND

☐ 11 bears
☐ A kangaroo
☐ Two astronauts
☐ A magic star wand

WISE CRACKS

Wizard Whitebeard has cast a happy spell! This scroll is inscribed with lots of jokes. Which one makes you laugh the most?

WHAT'S SO SPECIAL ABOUT THE WAY WIZARDS SERVE THEIR TEA?

THEY GIVE YOU BISCUITS ON A FLYING SORCERER!

HOW MANY WIZARDS DOES IT TAKE TO CAST A SPELL OF INVISIBILITY?

I DON'T KNOW, I CAN'T SEE THEM!

HOW BEST TO DESCRIBE A WIZARD'S BOOK?

SPELL-BINDING!

WHY CAN'T WIZARDS CLEAN FLOORS?

BECAUSE THE WITCHES STOLE THEIR BROOMS!

WHAT DO YOU CALL A LAUGHING POTION?

MAKES-YOU-GIGGLE-A-LOT-IOUS!

MORE THINGS TO DO
* Make up your own joke in the space on the scroll and test it on your friends.
* Try out five different laughs!

STUPENDOUS SORCERERS! I'M STILL DISCOMBOBULATED ABOUT WHERE MY MAGIC SCROLL IS HIDING. I HOPE I DIDN'T TURN IT INVISIBLE! DID YOU SPOT IT AND THE IMPRESSIVE NUMBER OF BLUE-RIBBONED SCROLLS I CREATED?

I'VE CONJURED UP A RIDDLE CLUE TO FOCUS OUR MINDS: SEEK OUT A MAN WITH A LONG WHITE BEARD AND ABOVE HIM A HANGING SIGN. THE SCROLL IS BUT A WHISKER AWAY!

Whitebeard

Candle wax

A mermaid's tail

Green gloop

Wizard Whitebeard needs an able apprentice to find these special spell ingredients. Look through the book so far and gather them as fast as you can!

Dinosaur spines

A jest of lemon

Egg timer

WIZARD WHITEBEARD'S SCROLL CHECKLIST

Cast your eyes over Wizard Whitebeard's quest and find...

- ☐ Wizard Whitebeard in a boat
- ☐ Someone blowing a whistle
- ☐ A man wearing a bow tie
- ☐ A snake shaking maracas
- ☐ A flag with five faces
- ☐ A sea lion
- ☐ Nine gold crowns
- ☐ A windmill
- ☐ Someone rolling a die
- ☐ Three wicker baskets
- ☐ Four jumping fish
- ☐ A gargoyle breathing fire
- ☐ A toy in a teacup
- ☐ Three genies
- ☐ A zebra crossing
- ☐ A red man that has jumped through a shield
- ☐ A wishing well
- ☐ A skeleton

ONE LAST THING...

How many stars can you find in Wizard Whitebeard's chapter (the star bullet points in the *More Things To Do* boxes don't count)?

DISGUISE, DISGUISE!

Beware, here are twelve Odlaws but which is the real one? Remember, Odlaw is pictured on the previous page if you need some help!

MORE THINGS TO DO

* Colour in the Odlaws!

* Can you spot something odd about the pattern on the frame?

SUPER SNEAKY SEA GAZING GAME

Odlaw loves to look out at sea with his pirate friends. Study the scene *very* closely and spot those of them noted in the ship's logbook below.

☐ Three men wearing skull and crossbones T-shirts

☐ Two men wearing hats with green feathers

☐ Three men with yellow beards

☐ Four men wearing red-and-white stripy trousers

☐ Three men wearing yellow bandanas with black spots

☐ Three men holding gold chalices

SUPER SNEAKY SEA GAZING GAME

How closely did you study Odlaw's pirate scene? Look through these binocular views and find them on the previous page.

RIDDLING RIDDLES AND TWISTY TONGUE TWISTERS

How many times can you repeat
**Black and yellow stripes –
Yellow and black stripes.**
without getting tongue-tied?

Can you decode this riddle
to find out who is keeping Odlaw
company aboard ship?
**My hands hang low
But my tail swings high,
See if you can spot me
Dangling in the sky.**

Repeat this sentence
five times and see how
tangled your tongue gets!
**Pirate Plunderers
Seek Scallywag
Scupperers.**

What am I?
**I have eight legs and two big eyes,
but don't look for me in the skies.**

TOP FIENDS

Meet Odlaw's most ferocious team of fiends. Look at the pictures on the trump cards and match them to the correct description.

Name: Hungry Growler

Lives: Swamps

Favourite Food: Everything and anything

Speed: Lumbering

Courage: 10

Spy Ability: 2

Fear Factor: 8

Special Skill: Roaring and emitting foul smells

Name: Heave Ho Henry

Lives: Dungeons

Favourite Food: Nuts and bolts

Speed: Slow when rusty

Courage: 4

Spy Ability: 9

Fear Factor: 10

Special Skill: Sneaking up on people

Name: Warty Gretel

Lives: The Witch's Castle

Favourite Food: Bats' tails, frogs' legs, eyes of a newt

Speed: Fast on a broom

Courage: 4

Spy Ability: 10

Fear Factor: 6

Special Skill: Potions and curses

Name: Captain Cutlass

Lives: The Black Skull ship

Favourite Food: Dried meats

Speed: Peg-leg slow

Courage: 9

Spy Ability: 6

Fear Factor: 6

Special Skill: Pillaging

MORE THINGS TO DO

* Who is your favourite fiend on this page?
* Who ranks the highest for their spying skills?
* Who is the most courageous?
* Who is the most terrifying?
* Who do you think would own a crystal ball?

SKULDUGGERY

Odlaw has muddled up the skull and crossbones flag!
Can you draw it in the right order in the grid below?

MORE THINGS TO FIND

Which one of Odlaw's villainous friends on this page has appeared somewhere else in this book?

Clue: It's a blood-curdling choice that will chill you to your bones!

SEA MONSTERS

Hear no evil, sea no evil! Colour in this monstrous lighthouse scene.
The pirates got a bit of shock when their ship sailed past it!

MORE THINGS TO FIND

☐ Seven spotty sea dragons

☐ Nine ladders

☐ A sea dragon flying upside down

☐ A pirate in stripy clothes

☐ A sea dragon wearing flying goggles

SLIPPERY SEARCH

Using your finger, trace a path through the tunnels to help Odlaw escape
and pick up his slithery black-and-yellow striped companion on the way.

MAGNIFIED MISCHIEF

Which one of Odlaw's magnifying lenses reveals
sneaky snakes, spy birds and cheeky monkeys?

MORE THINGS TO FIND

- ☐ 11 piranhas
- ☐ Two gold crowns
- ☐ Three broken spears
- ☐ 11 blue hats
- ☐ A snake staff
- ☐ A black-and-white shield
- ☐ A man wearing a pirate hat

SNAKING WORDS

Read the clues and work out the answers by joining up the letters inside each frame without taking your pen off the paper!

Clue: A sea-travelling invader

N I
G K
V I

Clue: A sword-swishing soldier

E T E
K M E
S U R

Clue: A skeletal symbol used by pirates

K S S E B S
U A N N O S
L L D C R O

MORE THINGS TO FIND

☐ Ten yellow-headed birds

☐ Three Draculas

☐ A flying witch

☐ Frankenstein's monster

☐ A pirate woman

SWASHBUCKLING CHAOS

Can you complete this jigsaw? Watch out there's a rogue piece! You could photocopy the page, cut out the pieces and make the real thing.

MORE THINGS TO FIND

☐ A scene in one jigsaw piece that is repeated elsewhere in the book

☐ Two musketeers with green faces

☐ A chequered flag

☐ Six musketeers wearing blue crested tunics

☐ A musketeer dog statue

☐ A green sedan

SNAKES AND LADDERS

Wally and Odlaw are playing snakes and ladders!
Follow the instructions to work out who wins.

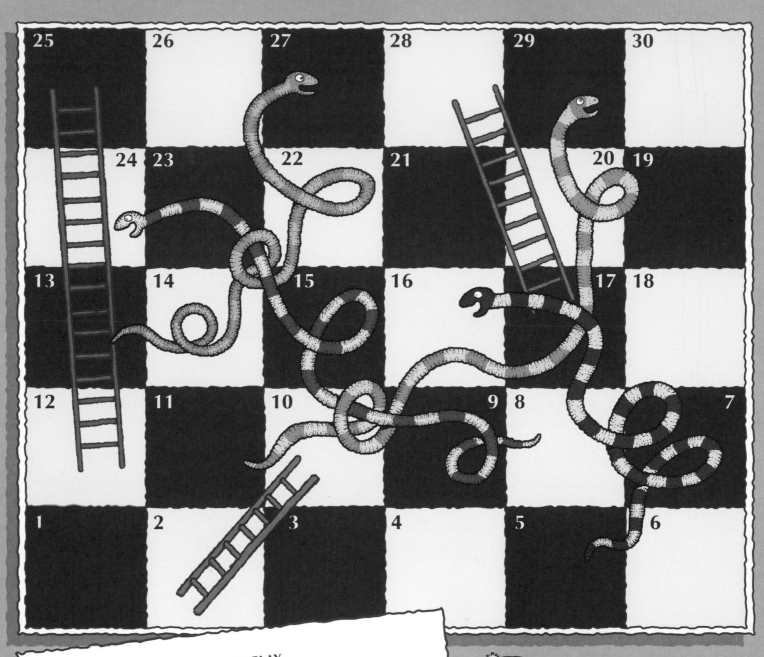

HOW TO PLAY

○ Look at the pictures of the dice. Odlaw's die is yellow and Wally's die is red.

○ Count the number of moves for each character on the board that their die shows.

○ If he lands on a square at the bottom of a ladder, go up it.

○ If he lands on a square with a snake's head, slide down it.

○ The winner is the player who lands on square number 30.

90

MORE THINGS TO DO

Find a die and play your own game of Snakes and Ladders with your friends.

FLIP FLOP SILHOUETTES

Sit opposite a friend, so you both have a scene facing you. See who can match the silhouettes from their logbook to their scene first – but beware, only four silhouettes appear in each scene!

LAND AHOY!

Study the pictures of the extraordinary lands Odlaw has sailed to and fill in the answers to each question below.

How many yellow birds?

_____

How many yellow custard pies have been thrown?

_____

How many black sunglasses?

_____

How many yellow-coloured balls?

_____

How many yellow fish?

_____

How many sleeves with black and yellow stripes?

_____

MORE THINGS TO DO

Add up all your answers to the questions above and turn to that page number. Can you spot Odlaw's yellow-and-black luggage label?

How many black moustaches?

_____

PIRATEY PUZZLE

Ahoy there! Fill in the answers next to these questions to reveal a word going downwards that is Odlaw's favourite piece of piratey disguise!

The ... seas (*clue: number of days in a week*)

Observing in secret

The rear part of a ship

Person in charge of the ship and its crew

Odlaw's treasure-hunting shipmates

Message in a ......

Heavy weight on rope keeping a ship in one place

Pieces of ..... (*clue: a number between 7 and 9*)

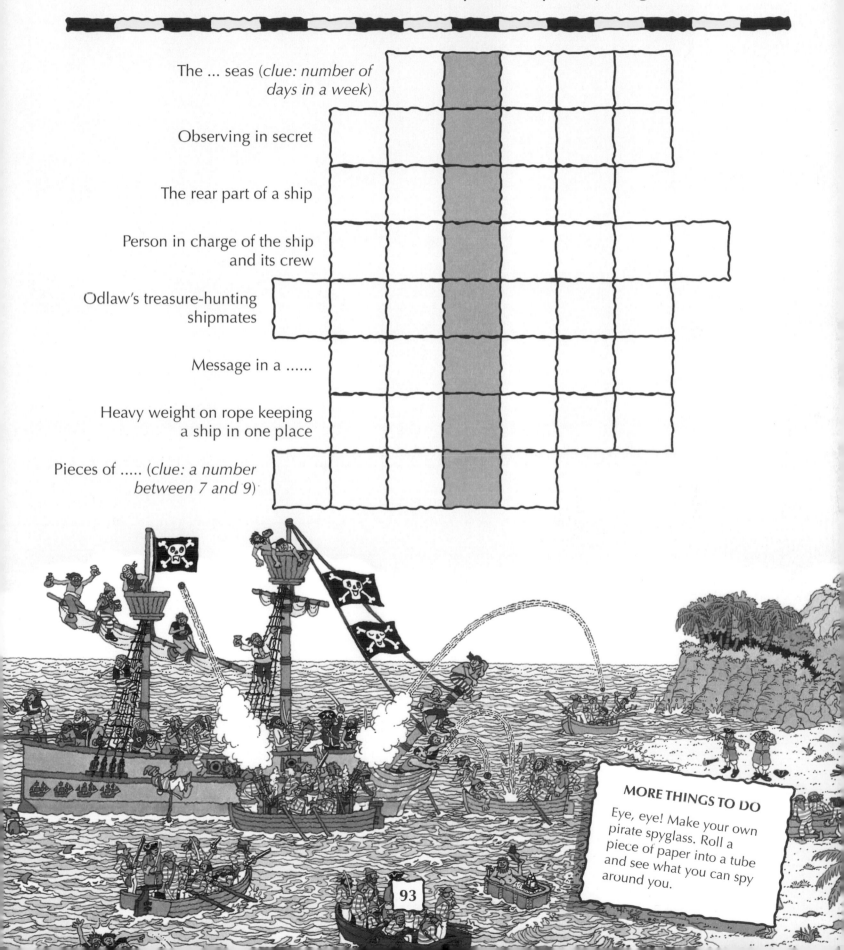

MORE THINGS TO DO

Eye, eye! Make your own pirate spyglass. Roll a piece of paper into a tube and see what you can spy around you.

WHAT A CATCH!

Odlaw's fishing for treasure. Untangle the lines to find out what he has caught on the end of his rod.

MORE THINGS TO FIND

- [ ] A fishing fish
- [ ] Two spotty fish
- [ ] Kissing fish

SWAMPY SWIRL

Read Odlaw's swampy, swirly message by turning the page in an anti-clockwise direction. Watch out, the message is written backwards!

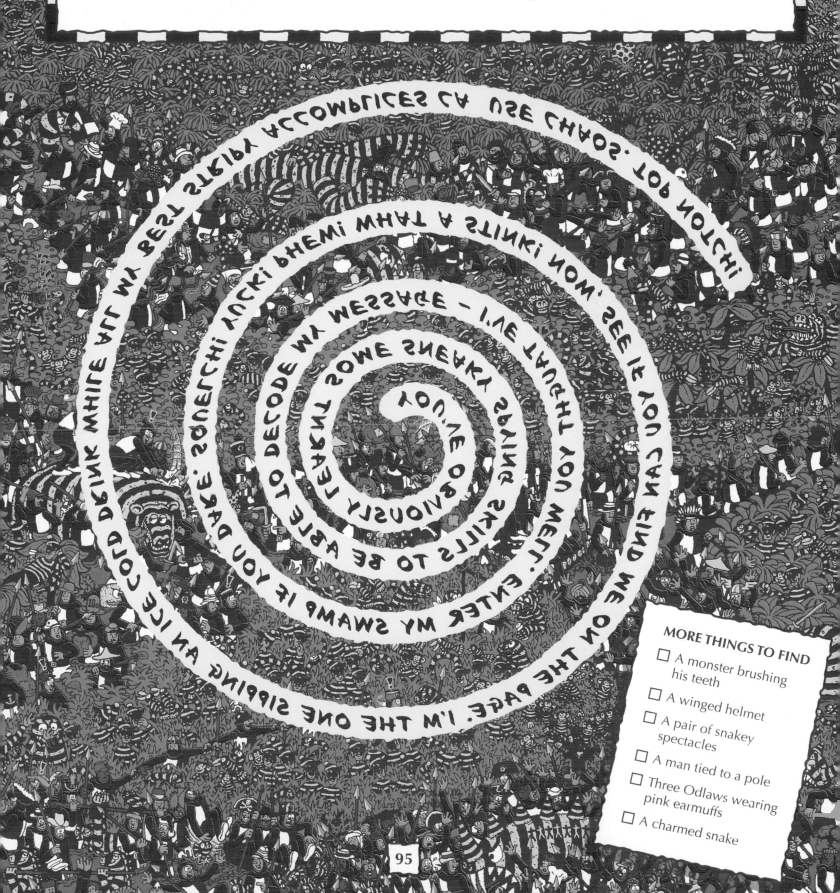

MORE THINGS TO FIND

- ☐ A monster brushing his teeth
- ☐ A winged helmet
- ☐ A pair of snakey spectacles
- ☐ A man tied to a pole
- ☐ Three Odlaws wearing pink earmuffs
- ☐ A charmed snake

BY MY CALCULATIONS, WE'RE NORTH OF NOWHERE UNLESS YOU'VE FOUND MY BINOCULARS. I'VE BARTERED WITH THE CAPTAIN FOR THIS CLUE, BUT I HOPE YOU KNOW HOW TO SPEAK PIRATE:

"AVAST! YE LANDLOCKED LUBBERS WILL BE SENT ON A BILGE-SUCKING SHANTY UNLESS YE HEAVE HO AND PILLAGE THE DARKEST TUNNELS TO UNCOVER ME MATIE'S BINOCULARS."

Odlaw

Can you spot where these pictures come from in Odlaw's chapter? Be careful, one is from somewhere else in the book!

ODLAW'S BINOCULARS CHECKLIST

Wait, there's more! Look back through the pictures and find...

☐ A boy dangling a spider from a stick

☐ An Odlaw wearing wellington boots

☐ Two swordfish

☐ Four black vultures

☐ A human weighing scales

☐ An angry musketeer

☐ Two yellow-and-black stripy top hats

☐ A seabed

☐ Eight sharks waiting for their dinner

☐ A red monster

☐ A man in a bath boat

ONE LAST THING...

Remember the four silhouettes on page 91 that you couldn't find... One silhouette in each logbook appears in your player's scene opposite. The remaining one in each logbook appears elsewhere in this book.

THAT WAS EPIC, WELL DONE! THANKS FOR TRACKING DOWN OUR PRECIOUS THINGS – WE'D BE LOST WITHOUT THEM. HA, HA!

THERE ARE ANSWERS TO SOME OF THE TRICKIEST PUZZLES OVER THE PAGE. DON'T GIVE UP ON THE OTHERS – ASK YOUR FRIENDS TO HELP IF YOU ARE STUCK.

THE ADVENTURE ISN'T OVER QUITE YET! REMEMBER GATHERING THE INGREDIENTS FOR WIZARD WHITEBEARD'S SPELL..? IT CREATED SEVERAL RARE GOLDEN SEALS, THE NUMBER OF WHICH IS REVEALED ON PAGE 76. CAN YOU FIND THEM BEFORE ODLAW'S PIRATE FRIENDS GET THERE FIRST?

HAPPY HUNTING!

Wally

ANSWERS

★ WALLY'S KEY ★

Pg 8 TRAVEL ESSENTIALS

MORE THINGS TO DO
usdartc epi = custard pie; dre eons = red nose;
niuylecc = unicycle

Pg 10 RED NOSE RUNAROUND

This is the shortest route.

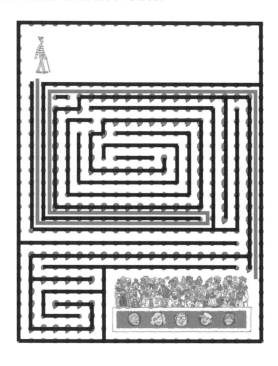

Pg 14 PYRAMID PUZZLE

MORE THINGS TO FIND
There are 121 triangles in the puzzle.

Pg 17 MOON MAZE MAYHEM

Pg 19 BALLOON BEDLAM

MORE THINGS TO DO
The missing pattern is the spotty balloon.

Pg 20 WILD AND WACKY W'S

Pg 21 SILLY STAMP SNAP

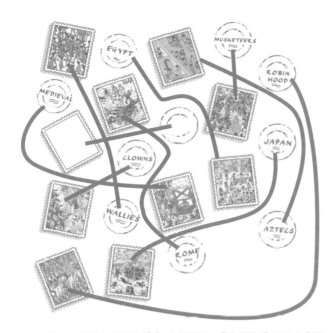

Pg 24 WALLY'S KEY CHECKLIST

Page 13 has the most number of red noses.

★ WOOF'S BONE ★

Pg 26 WAG TAIL WAY OUT

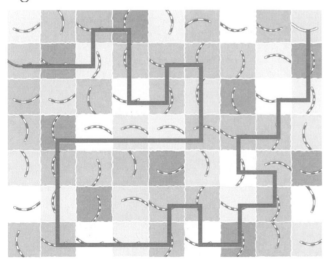

Pg 28 WHO'S WHO?

Pg 31 CONNECT THE BONES

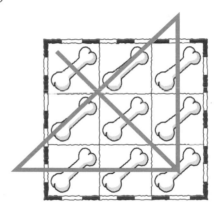

MORE THINGS TO DO

14 squares make up the grid.

Pg 32 FLOWER POWER

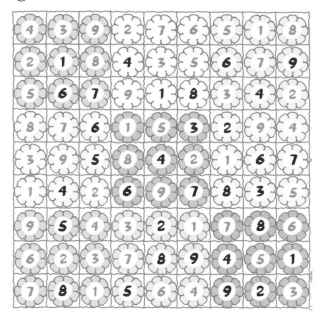

Pg 33 BULL'S EYE!

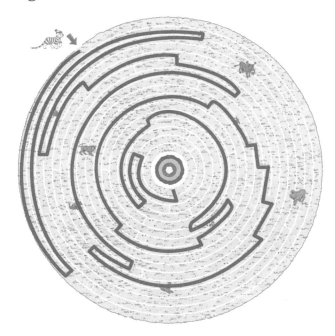

Pg 34 WOOF'S WORD WHEEL

It's as hard as rock – stone; *Woof's favourite thing* – bone; *Use to sniff* – nose; *Heads, shoulders, knees and ...* – toes; *Woof is one of these* – dog

Pg 35 TRUTH OR TAILS?

1. True; 2. False: answer, Parasaurolophus; 3. True; 4. True; 5. False: answer, their diet – herbivores eat vegetation and carnivores eat meat; 6. True: Tyrannosaurus rex; 7. True; 8. False: it had two wings; 9. True; 10. True

ONE MORE THING
Stegosaurus

Pg 37 DIGGING FOR GOLD

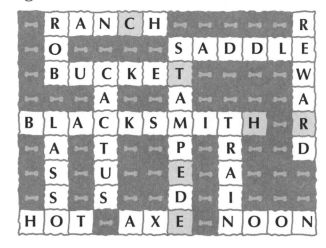

MORE THINGS TO DO
c / three

Pg 38 NUMBER CRUNCHING

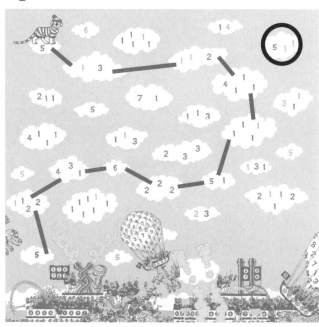

MORE THINGS TO DO
The circled cloud has the highest value.

Pg 39 DOG'S DINNER

Ready, steady, go! The race is on! Me and my canine friends are chasing our favourite food groups – sausages, bones, cats and even postmen!

MORE THINGS TO FIND
There are eight wow words.

Pg 41 PLAY BALL

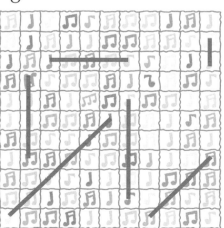

★WENDA'S CAMERA★

Pg 47 BUSY BANDSTAND

Drum – sticks; clarinet – reed; conductor – baton; trombone – mouthpiece; violin – bow; triangle – rod; piano – keys

Wenda's favourite song is *Walking in a Winter Wonderland*.

Pg 48 A COLOURFUL TUNE

Pg 50 WOBBLY WORD LADDERS

Wow; Now; Not; Dot
Song; Sing; King; Kind; Find

Pg 54 COSTUME COSTS

1 hat	£1
1 tie	£2
1 tie	£2
1 shirt	£3
1 shirt	£3
1 jacket	£4
=	£15

Pg 55 BOX BAMBOOZLE

MORE THINGS TO DO
The cube has seven other three-sided combinations. (Eight in total.)

Pg 56 OH CRUMBS!

eggs; butter; self raising flour; chocolate chips; icing sugar; red cherries; custard

Pg 59 DANCING SILHOUETTES

MORE THINGS TO FIND
Wenda's favourite dance is the waltz.

WIZARD WHITEBEARD'S ★ SCROLL ★

Pg 62 STARS AND STRIPES

The path marked in yellow leads to Wizard Whitebeard's star.

MORE THINGS TO FIND
The path in blue crosses the most paths.

Pg 63 SOMETHING FISHY

Pg 64 SPELL-TACULAR!

Magic makes much mayhem

Pg 65 GIANT GAME

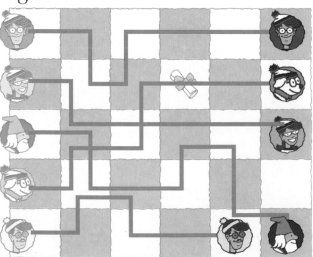

Pg 66 MIX-UP MADNESS

Pg 68 WORD CASTLE

R	O	F		A	R	A	M	I	D		A	X	E
M	X	A		J	O	P	W	W	O		W	G	R
L	W	A		D	R	A	W	B	R	I	D	G	E	H	L	D	R	A
F	L	A	G	L	V	N	E	K	R	C	A	T	A	P	U	L	T
N	T	P	C	A	S	T	L	E	L	Q	P	U	F	M	P	X	E
W	Q	T	E	U	F	Y	U	X	H	D	A	B	A	T	T	L	E
M	O	A	T	H	Y	K	W	S	E	J	I	U	L	E	I	A	F
D	G	E	M	I	L	A	I	N	S	I	F	O	R	T	A	F	R
A	R	R	O	W	H	R	E	E	A	K	L	K	C	E	T	L	H
H	F	M	A	R	A	W	N	P	M	T	L	H	F	L	A	G	T
W	A	L	L	T	O	H	Y	O	E	A	B	O	W	P	P	C	G

MORE THINGS TO FIND
The two magic words are 'Open Sesame'.

Pg 70 GENIE-OUS!

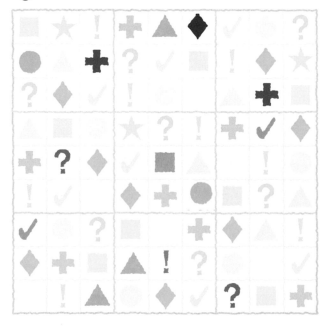

Pg 72 FRUIT SQUASH

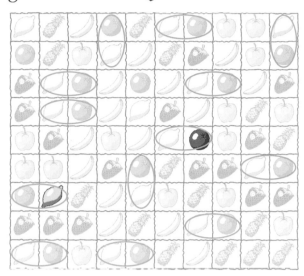

Pg 75 WHICH WITCH IS WHICH?

1. Mystic Martha plays a brilliant broom tune.
2. Noisy Norma likes to wake the dead.
3. Wicked Wartie wears a cloak at night, and its colour rhymes with fright.
4. Tangle Toes Tina trips everywhere she goes.
5. Moorb Hctiw rides her broom in a peculiar way.

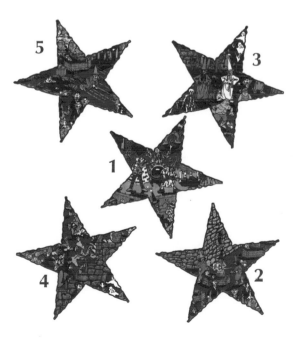

Pg 76 MAGIC NUMBER
The magic number is 5.

★ ODLAW'S ★ BINOCULARS

Pg 83 TOP FIENDS

Warty Gretel   Heave Ho Henry   Captain Cutlass   Hungry Growler

MORE THINGS TO DO
Highest spying skills: Warty Gretel
Most courageous: Hungry Growler
Most terrifying: Heave Ho Henry
Crystal Ball: Warty Gretel

Pg 84 SKULDUGGERY

Pg 86 SLIPPERY SEARCH

Pg 88 SNAKING WORDS

A sea travelling invader – viking; *A sword-swishing soldier* – musketeer; *A skeletal symbol used by pirates* – skull and crossbones

Pg 90 SNAKES AND LADDERS

Wally wins the game!
His first move takes him to square 4
second move: to square 10
third move: to square 25 (up a ladder)
fourth move: to square 13 (down a snake)
fifth move: to square 28 (up a ladder)
sixth move: to square 30

Pg 92 LAND AHOY!

7 yellow birds; 5 black sunglasses; 6 yellow
fish; 7 yellow custard pies; 11 yellow balls;
5 black-and-yellow striped sleeves; 8 black
moustaches = page 49

Pg 93 PIRATEY PUZZLE

```
  S E V E N
S P Y I N G
S T E R N
C A P T A I N
P I R A T E S
B O T T L E
A N C H O R
E I G H T
```

Pg 94 WHAT A CATCH!

Pg 95 SWAMPY SWIRL

You've obviously learnt some sneaky spying
skills to be able to decode my message –
I've taught you well. Enter my swamp if you
dare. Squelch! Yuck! Phew! What a pong!
Now, see if you can find me on the page.
I'm the one sipping an ice cold drink while
all my best stripy accomplices cause chaos.
Top notch!

ONE LAST THING...

Did you ever see Wally, Woof
(but only his tail), Wenda,
Wizard Whitebeard and Odlaw
roaming outside their chapters
in this book? See if you can find
them if you didn't spot them
first time round.